When life tricked me..

Vikarant khanna is a sailor by profession and writer by passion. He is an avid guitarist and fond of composing songs. This is his first book.

When life tricked me..

and love kicked me...

Vikrant Khanna

Srishti
Publishers & Distributors

Srishti Publishers & Distributors
N-16, C. R. Park
New Delhi 110 019
editorial@srishtipublishers.com

First published by
Srishti Publishers & Distributors in 2011

10 9 8 7 6 5 4 3

Dedicated to all my friends and girlfriends whose real life experiences contributed in creating this book.

Acknowledgements

I like to thank all those who read, contributed, appreciated and criticised my manuscript all this while and helped me towards its completion. A special thanks to my dear friend Nuru and sister Guddu for their valuable inputs and sharp criticism, my parents for their unconditional love and support throughout, my editor at Srishti Publishers who after my many importunings finally conceded in publishing this book.

And above all, I like to thank my profession for giving me those peaceful and uninterrupted times in the middle of all the beautiful oceans of the world. Had it not been to the tranquility of nature and my boredom, I would not have got nostalgic about all those good and not so bad moments with my friends convincing me to pen them down and capture them in form of a book.

Prologue

The day had finally come for which Vikram Oberoi had long waited. It was a day he dreamt of living through innumerable nights. It was the day of his recognition, something he had always desired.

Today he was being rewarded.

But getting to it had been difficult, considering the laid back attitude that he once had towards life. The frivolous and trance-like attitude of his had been his trademark. Often criticized, but still accepted by his friend as there was a rakish coolness about him.

But life had other plans.

As he frittered through his life carelessly, one fateful day everything around him changed. Never before had he felt that sad and marooned. His world shook within him and made him a completely different person there he was now.

Vik, as he was commonly known by his friends, was a man in his mid twenties. He had sharp, riveting eyes that constantly surveyed; something they hadn't done much in the past. His mind, always pensive, planned to make the most out of life. His tall frame and rugged features gave him a slightly attractive appearance but he himself never seemed to notice it. He carried the persona of a man with a purpose, a quality embedded in him only recently.

When he awoke from his slumber, the sun had already set. Dusk was beginning to take control of the starry evening. The balmy chill outside characterized the month of November.

As he lay astretch on his bed, he felt both languorous and fresh at the same time. He thought about the previous year, how time evolved him as a person he never thought he would be. It had been a revelation in itself. And then he thought about today. He felt ecstatic. There was a self possessed smile on his face that somewhat managed to cloak the pain that he was now used to.

He got up from his bed and slouched on his favourite chair. The memories didn't seem to fade away. *One day I'll do something big to make you guys feel proud of me.*

He looked up to the pictures of his friends that he had put religiously on the wall. They were all there - Nirvaan, Ruheen, Purnima, Rachna and of course Raghav - his best friend.

It was to him he owed all his success.

An hour later he left his house for the evening that awaited him.

1

THE LONG WAIT…

It was a bright Wednesday morning of the first week of November. The sun just ascending in the morning sky that showed up resplendently with bright orange and red colours streaking across it. The birds squawking and chirping, just up from their slumber welcoming the morning. The air was filled with mist that left the trees moist. It was redolent of the ambrosial fragrance that New Delhi offered its inhabitants. The setting was distinctly verdant all over Defence Colony, in the southern part of this city.

Just then an alarm rang in E-46. A languid hand came out of the blanket rummaging for the alarm clock over the bed. Her name was Ruheen. Any other day she would have hated to do the same – to get up so early in the morning and get ready for work. But this day was different. She had been longing for this day for the last six months.

Ruheen was a young woman with a lithe, wiry figure with eyes that gleamed almost inexorably. Even without washing her face, she managed to look pretty. She carried herself with an exceptional air though never supercilious.

She got up from her bed immediately and made herself some coffee, then skittered toward the balcony, something she did every morning.

The balcony was minuscule, the size of a bathroom. It was laden with white marble tiles on the floor arranged disorderly. At the side were three wooden chairs sloping outwards with beige colour cushions that had some kind of a symbol embroidered on them with purple and red threads. Ruheen slouched on one of them.

She sipped her coffee savouring its rich aroma that took away her drowsiness. She looked up towards the reddish sky that was predominantly clear, admiring the beauty of nature that surrounded her.

It was a chilly morning, she observed as she brought her long arms close to her body to induce some warmth. Her mind, engaged in deep thoughts, about what she would be experiencing in the coming days. A bit apprehensive of the future though, she managed to carry a confident persona. She thought about the past six months, how she had been looking forward to this day. She thought about Nirvaan and got nostalgic about the past, of the days she spent with him – how for the first time in twenty six years of her life she had fallen in love.

It was a beautiful feeling that had filled her heart with unprecedented happiness. But along with it, there were a whole lot of complexities. The otherwise thoughtful Ruheen had become unstable. She got entangled in her own cobweb of possibilities. But she endured, for she knew she was in love the very first moment she saw him. And since then it had been a long wait, a wait that apparently ended today.

Finally, its time; she thought.

Just then, her roommate and closest friend Purnima joined her.

"Hi, morning." said Ruheen.

"Hey." Purnima drawled rubbing her eyes.

Purnima was very short and her hair was cut to her jaw. She had a splotchy complexion that appeared all the more dark owning to Kajal she used to religiously apply underneath her eyes. Her ears were jagged with four holes each, embedded with small round silver earrings that gave her something of a female rockstar look. The earrings kept changing with the day of the week and sometimes even with the time of a day. Her self-obsessiveness and continuous talking abilities were the two pillars of her identity. These qualities embedded in her were sky high as opposed to her 4 feet 10 inches height. Nonetheless, she was Ruheen's favourite person after Nirvaan.

Ruheen and Purnima had met 5 years ago. It was the first day of their degree course in Pearl – the fashion designing institute in West Delhi. Purnima had come to college in an autorickshaw. To her dismay she had left her purse at home – a place she temporarily shifted to after moving from Bangalore. She rummaged for it inside her huge leather bag – a size huge enough to accommodate her – but couldn't find it. She hated this incorrigible habit of forgetting things. It was something she had tried getting rid of, but had only managed aggravating it. The bulging eyes and sullen look on the driver's face made her condition only worse. She was not very fond of speaking to auto drivers – "they always eye you at the wrong places" she used to complain.

"Madamji are you giving me the money or not" the driver demanded.

Purnima observed his eyes whisked up and down measuring her petite figure. *Bloody sex starved moron.*

"Just hang on here." She blurted and sprang inside the college. Inside she rolled her eyes to find the best possible prey. Her line of sight passed over two twenty something guys, both shabbily dressed. Immediately she rejected them. *Poor guys I would have given them some money if I had my purse.* Next her eyes fell on a surd. He appeared to be a happy go lucky man. He wore a superman T-shirt that hoarded the line – "Proud to be a super surd", self righteously. God, what's with his dressing sense, she thought. Then she looked at her own clothes and allowed herself a smile of pride. Next she looked at a female who was busy on her phone. Purnima observed she had a very pleasant looking face with a supple figure. She was Ruheen.

"That's my girl." She set forth her best possible stride towards her that she was capable of, but her small feet offered little help.

"Hey there, could you lend me some money?" She had squealed and then she introduced herself.

Later that day they met again and confabulated for hours. They loved each other's company and immediately became friends. Both of them had found each other of the same genre, excessively fond of talking. In the evening Ruheen inquired about her whereabouts and Purnima replied that she was still looking for a decent place to move in.

"So why don't you move in with me?" Ruheen offered virtuously. Purnima accepted her proposal a second later.

And since then they had been together. They were best friends and always privy to all the secrets in each other's lives. They complimented and understood each other well. Howsoever besieging life got, they found solace only by talking it out with each other something they could do for hours. Their conversations normally began in the morning before getting ready for office. The topics included but were never limited to – office, their boss, colleagues, guys, good boyfriends, bad boyfriends, good husbands, bad husbands, dressing sense of people, general insidious remarks and sundry to mention a very few. They would haul and yank the topic for hours till nothing was left in it. Ironically, the conclusion to all their topics was always the same – "Oh just let it be, these guys."

"Hey somebody's got a smile on her face." Purnima yawned rubbing her moisture laden eyes.

Ruheen's smile widened.

"So he's coming back today, huh ?"

"Yeah after six long months."

"Good, make sure you kick his ass big this time."

"Sure I will, God save that dog now." Ruheen replied through clenched teeth.

Ruheen thought about Nirvaan – how cleverly he had evaded all her questions last time. "I need more time to be sure." was his answer to all her questions.

Well this time I would be needing more than that, she decided.

"All right then, I'm off to the washroom then, got to wake up

Rachna also." Purnima said as she left the balcony.

The third member of their house was Rachna. She was the sort of girl who carried her heart on her sleeve and was unmistakably proud of it. She had a perfect round face with thick curly black rebellious hair. Her eyes equally round, sparkled with an exceptional confidence. Her cheeks were flecked with tiny freckles. She had an unpleasant flabby body with an equally unpleasant paunch that protruded when she wore tight tops occasionally bought from the tacky Sarojini Nagar Market on Sundays.

Unlike the other two girls in the apartment, Rachna needed a measly twenty minutes to get ready for office. This, however, did not include the *big job* in the loo as she did not find comfort in splaying her big fat legs on the Indian style shit pot. She preferred the loo of her office that was adorned with ritzy Italian marbles, breathtaking state of the art décor and opulent lights that exuded votive luminosity. The shit bowl itself, was very mesmerizing – it had a rich porcelain finish with its seat as soft as a cushion. Rachna spent the first twenty minutes of her office on it. Not that nature did not call upon her when she was home but she preferred to control the nature's outburst even in the forty five minutes cab ride from Defence Colony to Gurgaon and finally letting it off there. She had always been very infamous for the intoxicating smell that she endowed upon her cab mates leaving them with their noses pressed throughout the ride.

When Purnima entered her room she was struck by an intense wave of nausea. It seemed to her that an earthquake or a similar natural calamity had struck the room. "Gosh, her room is so messy." she exclaimed, as she herself was very fastidious about cleanliness.

The room was a measly eight by eight feet. The walls were covered with a pale yellow colour with a single light arched on the right side top corner that gave the room a very soporific feel. There was no bed sheet on the bed and it was vastly occupied by dirty linen apart from the five feet three inches, eighty five kilos Rachna.

Purnima fed the little solitary fish in the small circular vase over the table. The amphibian was a small, rich yellow coloured fish with bright orange and red patterns neatly carved on its body. She was a very restless creature, panting and pounding through the water the entire day. Her ruby red eyes whisked through the entire room constantly as though surveying it. She was Rachna's favourite pal and she fondly called her Mishi.

Rachna had this uncanny habit of talking her life out to her who in turn scrolled her eyes sideways as though understanding her. It had always been hard to fathom for the people who know Rachna about such a futile thing as talking to your pet, but Rachna always had the same answer, "to find peace, you must always be heard well and Mishi is by far the best listener I have ever known."

Averting her gaze from the filthy room as though oblivious to her surroundings, Purnima tried waking Rachna. After ten minutes of arduous calling and beckoning, Rachna finally woke up. With a slight raise of her brow towards Purnima, she scurried towards the bathroom. Purnima went in the opposite direction towards her wardrobe and girded herself for the most challenging and toughest job of the day – 'deciding what to wear to office.'

Ruheen was still outside on the balcony sipping the last bit of her coffee. She looked up at the cumulus clouds with their subtle movement. They looked beautiful with the sun lending its rich kaleidoscopic colours. Ruheen's eyes gleamed with an exceptional luminosity that characterized the glow on her face which was missing for the past few months. She felt a trickle behind her neck and cocked her head gleefully. Her heart was pounding in tandem with her mind that was an ocean of thoughts. She felt wonderful. A minute later, she sighed deeply, got up from the chair and went into the living room.

Adjoining the two metre wide balcony was the living room. It was unlike the other rooms in the society that were ostentatiously decorated as though expecting guests every evening. It was truncated into a bedroom cum living room. At the far side of the room were two quaint teak wooden beds facing each other in such a way that the passage was left unobscured for the other rooms. In most houses in South Delhi, this arrangement of rooms was not very uncommon with a single passage in a straight line connecting all rooms leaving its inhabitants with an iota of privacy.

When Ruheen entered the room, Purnima appeared lost in a maze of thoughts. Her mind was busy selecting the best clothes that would match the day of the week. It was always a difficult decision. She held a long comb with which she brushed her hair constantly. She had a thing for them and regarded one's hair as one's husband. While describing a person, she would always start from the hair. Quite often, in her description, the person with the best hair turned out to be the person with the best character.

"Purnima come on hurry up, we can't afford to be late today, it would be the fifth consecutive day otherwise" Ruheen commented.

She herself was only slightly better when it came to time management.

The cab- a white coloured Tavera, arrived twenty minutes late at half past seven. After waiting for another ten minutes, the driver couldn't help honking relentlessly and wondered even after his delay what was holding the girls. The girls, as usual were engaged in the last minute lookout at the mirror. There was something about her few hair strands that didn't seem to be in place which Purnima was trying to address.

As the honking grew louder all three of them ran towards the door. After locking, it occurred to Purnima, her phone was left behind.

"Gosh Pooh" both of them screamed, "the pussy that you are".

The door was opened again and Purnima sprinted inside. Meanwhile the driver gave up. Stupefied, he shut the engines, slid his seat back and prepared himself for a short nap. Upstairs, Purnima was inside a second time searching for her wallet. And then the third time for her make-up kit.

After reprising her daily routine thrice, Purnima finally came out to the rueful grin of Ruheen and Rachna. They rushed towards the cab as though waiting for it the entire morning. The driver got up from his nap on hearing the babbling of girls and opened the back door for them.

"What Madams late come again?" he complained through an expression that didn't expect a justified answer.

True to his expectations, the three of them ignored him as though getting late were their birthright.

Inside, the other passengers pressed their noses tight as Rachna entered the cab as she eyed them with disdain.

2

"KAZI" - *THE FIGHTER*

They reached the office at half past eight, thirty minutes behind their daily schedule. The cab driver drove the car in a frenzied rush zigzagging through the morning traffic. As soon as the car came to a halt, the doors were opened and Rachna's cab mates cavorted outside as their lungs gasped for fresh air not intoxicated with her natural whiffs. Rachna needed to see the loo immediately.

As she set herself towards her favourite morning destination, Purnima inquired scornfully "Rachna where to?" Rachna shrugged and passed a middle finger sign before sprinting inside, something she desired for the last hour, abusing the hideous traffic in front of them.

They worked in an Indian retail company 'Silhouettes and Styles', in short SnS, all three of them. Ruheen was a senior merchandiser Purnima and Rachna her subordinates. The building was huge, on a road perpendicular to the National Highway-8 that connected Delhi to Gurgaon. Inside, the design of the office was grandiose. It was laden with Italian marbles that gleamed in sheer symphony. The lights on the ceiling were bright, encapsulated in little rectangular covers that imparted exceptional luminosity enlivening the frayed atmosphere. The ambience of the place was very soothing and it somewhat abated the encumbrance of the deadlines that the staff had to meet.

They occupied their respective tables and worked on the computer for their morning mails. Ruheen's fingers worked lazily as opposed to Purnima's who was in love with the computer and everything associated with it.

Ten minutes later, a rather subdued and energetic Rachna turned up at her seat to the smirking glances of her friends. Peace oozed from her as she separated herself from the huge lump in her stomach.

"Fuck you bitch." she growled at Purnima who was smirking at her from her table.

As Ruheen worked her spidery fingers through the computer, she was summoned to her boss' cabin. His cabin was on the far end, right hand corner of the room emblazoned with glass walls that offered him a panoramic view of his staff, leaving them with absolutely no chance of any eerie, discreet work as they were always apprehensive that big brother might be watching.

When Ruheen entered his cabin, he was busy on his phone. She worked her hazel-green eyes through the room with a premonition that something was going to trouble her today; on a day when she never wanted to work, just bask in the office.

Mr. Farooq Altaf Hussain Kazi was in his late fifties. He wore the expression of a man who was constantly snapped by the world. The angry, sullen look on his face was almost permanent. When he entered the office he never greeted anyone. On the contrary, when somebody wished him he had his trademark 'why the hell are you wishing me' look on his face. Gradually his staff avoided greeting him. The constant dirty look on his face was as if world war three had begun between him and the rest of the world. With immense hatred and ire his staff had termed him *"Kazi the fighter"*. A smile seldom lit his face up and when it did, it was the biggest gossip of the day.

"You know what! I saw a smile on the *fighter's* face today."

"Phew, unbelievable."

At that age his hair and moustache were jet black, darker than that of a 20 year old. Thanks to the black dye he coloured them with on a weekly basis. His staff noted that it made him look all the more ugly.

When he hung up on his phone, Ruheen observed a subtle quiver in his moustache, which in itself was a dangerous sign. She had learnt from her past experience that a slight movement of his moustache was the equivalent of a high-tech plan welling in his all the more dark mind.

I'm screwed today, she thought.

"Sit down:" *the fighter* ordered.

"Sir."

Ruheen pulled a chair and prepared herself for a long monotonous speech.

"Nothing" *the fighter* admonished, "Absolutely nothing is

happening as per my plan."

Ruheen noticed that the colour of his eyes changed from a pale white to a bright red. She sat motionless.

"I am the boss, I will decide what is to be done here, I will sack all employees if I don't see profits, I will ...." the furious look on his face was similar to Sunny Deol on his way to smash a hundred people together.

"You bloody youngsters! When I was your age, I never took any offs, I worked on Saturdays & Sundays also, I never went out for any vacation, I worked all day and night."

He took a break, drank some water and resumed. "Hell, I didn't even make any friends so that I could concentrate on my work."

"Yes Sir."

"I was a workaholic, never went out for movies or partying."

"Yes Sir."

"You know I was the best employee of my company."

"Yes Sir."

"And look at you guys, bloody youngsters, want to do everything in life and not work."

"Yes sir."

Ruheen wasn't listening to him, she sat there merely counting the I's and My's he used.

In a few minutes, she lost count of them.

The next two hours passed in over ambitious plans, cheeky comparisons, laborious marketing strategies, past regretting, lengthy presentations. As *the fighter* flung tattering words at Ruheen, she found herself drowning in them without a life jacket; the more she struggled to come to the surface, the more the whirlpool of words sucked her. It was a nothing but a struggle – to spend a solitary two hours with *the fighter*, unarmed, in his cabin.

When she came out, she was distraught and in a state of distress. She found solace in the open space away from the claustrophobic cabin of Mr. Kazi that echoed with his churlish big talks. Her mind was clouded with Nirvaan's thoughts.

As she walked in the passage leading to her chair, she observed the affable Purnima busy stroking the keyboard, so hard that it always made her little fingers red. Her legs were so short that they didn't touch the floor, just hung in mid air. Ruheen smiled looking at her, the first in the last two hours, and passed her a flying kiss. On her seat, she tried concentrating on work but Nirvaan never allowed her to. He occupied her mind so much that nothing could replace it.

A few minutes later, she heard Rachna ranting on her phone behind her. Immediately Ruheen knew who it was on the other end.

"I broke up with that bastard." Rachna said as she came towards Ruheen's desk to share her agony.

"But why? didn't you guys meet just 2 weeks back?"

"Yeah, I know but this asshole is not fond of drinking, what am I supposed to do with a teetotaller like him." She replied with an air of contempt and disapproval before scrambling out for a smoke.

Ruheen nodded quietly. If she recalled correctly that was Rachna's fifth breakup in the last two months. Although she disliked the flirt in her, she kind of secretly admired her attitude towards guys – "use them or they'll use you." Her idea of dating a guy only meant fun. Hell, life to her was only meant for fun. She never compromised on that, then be the stakes against work, friends or life. And the road that led her to fun always began with an alcoholic rhapsody. After her house, the next place where she spent most of her time were the clubs, bars and pubs.

'Way to go girl' Ruheen mused.

Seconds later Nirvaan was back, back in her mind. She smiled lovingly as she commemorated the part. Time took her back to that day when she first met him. It was the day that changed her life forever in a few seconds.

3

LUST AT FIRST SIGHT...

It was one of those nights that was awaited for the entire week by the youth of Delhi. After working for long and hard hours in the office, it always came down to Saturday for partying. Night life has evolved considerably in Delhi in the last couple of years owing to the progress of its NCR with places like Gurgaon and Noida becoming the crowd bustling party hubs.

In E-46 however, the party had begun early with Rachna giving in to her alcoholic cravings since afternoon. She was listening to Pink Floyd and was *comfortably numb*. She had called her three friends to their place from where they planned to head for the disc Elevate in the Centrestage Mall in Noida.

"Three guys are coming, Wow." Purnima had salivated when Rachna told them about the night's plan.

"But who are these guys?" Ruheen inquired.

"Oh just some old friends." Rachna replied disinterestedly, slightly inebriated.

"Tell us their names at least." Purnima asked with a hint of annoyance in her voice caused by her disinterest.

"Alright, okay, relax; one of them is Raghav, then there is Vik and the third is Nirvaan." she replied in an alcoholic haze.

"Oh nice." Purnima was thrilled and her annoyance disappeared like white smoke in air.

"Oh and please be careful, don't look too hard at them," Rachna warned, "especially this Nirvaan, he is the biggest flirt I know."

"Of course." both of them replied in perfect togetherness with umpteen disregard to her advice as though they were the smartest females on the planet.

Months later, Ruheen wished she had taken the advice seriously.

A few minutes after Rachna's advice, they sat glued to their respective wardrobes, heads muzzled as they braced themselves for one of the hardest tasks. They tried various combinations and finally reached a decision in a few hours. However, when finally dressed and ready for the night, clouds of doubt hovered over them. They wanted to change a part of, or may be the entire attire. The initial discussion, however, made headway in the direction of Ruheen's ear rings.

"Are the little blue beads in the pocket of the bronze rings matching with the shade of the dark blue of my jeans?"

"Yeah, may be; but not with the black top I think, what say?"

"Oh and what about those silver round earrings I got from Janpath the other day, they certainly don't need any matching."

"Yes, but I don't think they match the occasion."

"Hmmm…. right, but what about those small black ones, they should definitely be fine, I think so………."

"No, they got that little pink spot in the centre, they'll never match with your sandals, come on, what you talking?"

"Fuck!"

And the decision had to take into consideration the day of the week, the month of the year, the party place, the fact that it was their first meeting with the three guys. It was anything, but a simple decision.

An hour later, Rachna came running to their room. "Girls, let's go they have come."

"No" both screamed uproariously "we are not ready yet."

After fifteen minutes, the guys became impatient and honked persistently. "God, these girls, always."

The girls, finally did manage to come but not without the last minute rush. Purnima, of course, did her usual three rounds of in and out of the house. The forgotten items were the lip gloss, mascara, nail enamel in that order.

Before getting close to them, Rachna warned again, "Remember – don't look too hard, especially Nirvaan – biggest and best flirt." she spoke monosyllabically.

"Alright! we know."

The guys were thrilled to see them after the apprehension that the doors to the club would be shut if they waited a little longer.

Rachna did the honours of the introduction. Vikram was tall with a lean frame and both Ruheen and Purnima found him slightly attractive. Raghav appeared to be in his mid twenties. He carried the expression of a person who was treated well by the world. He was a few inches shorter than six feet. His eyes glistened and a jaunty smile never left his face. There was an air of gaiety and confidence about him. When he spoke, all ears listened for he always made sense.

But it was Nirvaan who stole all eyes, in particular of Ruheen. He was the sort of guy that every girl desired, at least for the looks. His tall muscular frame, chiselled features, the casual lock of hair gave him the appearance of a fashion model. His rhetoric was even more endearing, particularly when it came to impressing girls. Ruheen, with the advice long forgotten, appeared vastly impressed. Nirvaan too, was struck by her pristine beauty.

It had just been twice when their eyes locked together, momentarily, yet there was this uncanny feeling brooding somewhere inside them, that it was ages since they had known each other or maybe they were made to know each other for ages. Fleetingly, even with that distance between them there was this supernatural element that worked through them which made the world around them vanish. There was a substantial rise in their heartbeat and pulse and when it reached its pinnacle, they looked at each other again. And at that very moment, there was a whole lot of communication between those two pair of ignorant eyes in the dark.

"Alright people come on, I think it's time we all make a move." Raghav suggested.

All of them sat in Nirvaan's brand new Octavia, the girls took the back seat and the guys somehow managed in front with Nirvaan on the driver's seat.

"Fast. You have to be really fast Nirvaan if we want to get inside the disc today." Raghav said.

"Sure."

It was close to midnight when their car crossed the DND Flyway that connected Delhi to Noida. Nirvaan drove the car, exhilarated, swaying and swerving on the not so wide roads of Noida. Rachna had bought a bottle of whiskey in the car. Virtuously, she made drinks for everyone including the driver. Music played loud on the ritzy Blaupunkt speakers, the palpitation of which could be heard a long distance on the deserted roads, loud enough to snuff out the sleep of the occasional slum dwellers alongside the road.

Elevate was on the fifth floor of the Centre Stage Mail. It came alive after the midnight hours and soared until twilight. It had a body sonic dance floor that converted sound into vibrations. The breathtaking lighting and booming music offered a perfect partying experience.

They danced on the floor along with a horde of other people. Their bodies wiggled and twisted from side to side. It was one thing they all loved. A few hours later Purnima was alone on the dance floor. But she never realized it. She danced wildly as though the world was coming to an end. Often her little body was pushed and elbowed by the crowd but she remained trance-like, unaffected in her own world.

Vik, Raghav and Rachna came to the bar for drinks. They took pleasure in observing other people in their wild and sometimes puerile acts. After a few drinks, Raghav and Vik realized they were no competition to Rachna in terms of guzzling alcohol. They dealt in sips whereas she in glasses. They noticed even after drinking more than half a bottle booze since evening she stood firmly on the ground, her feet never wobbled. Not that they were beginners, but Rachna was no match.

"Somebody can drink." Vik announced.

Rachna looked at him, unperturbed, raised her middle finger and glugged another glass as if it was water.

He withdrew his gaze from hers. "Where are the others?" he asked quickly to change the topic.

"There." Raghav smiled, pointing towards Purnima who was enacting Shilpa Shetty's moves on Rihaana's 'Umbrella'.

"And Nirvaan, Ruheen?"

"Over there on the sofa."

Vik looked at them closely. He didn't move his eyes from them. A few seconds later, he started screaming "Hey guys! look at them, they are kissing" he paused to re-focus his eyes, "and oh my god so passionately."

Raghav moved his face casually to look at them. "I knew this was coming the first time they saw each other." he replied.

All eyes on the stage were glued on Nirvaan and Ruheen who had their tongue in each other's mouth. Nirvaan, as good as he always was, did his favourite act of shoving his hand up Ruheen's satin top as he felt her cup shaped breasts and squeezed them with sheer pleasure. His other hand drew her closer to him and then it slipped behind towards her pumpkin shaped ass caressing them fondly. Ruheen had her eyes shut as she gasped for breath in sheer ecstacy while Nirvaan's both hands worked through her silky smooth curves. Both were lost in a world of lust as they became oblivious to their surroundings. The thought of taking this to the next level and getting a room did occur to Nirvaan as he signalled towards the exit, but Ruheen's sudden retreat took him by surprise.

"Are these fuckers not meeting for the first time." Vik shrieked.

Rachna allowed herself another drink. Then smiled at her advice she gave Ruheen few hours back.

"The best and the biggest just got better and bigger."

4

SOUNDS LIKE A PLAN....

The 'Friends' theme blared on her Nokia N95 phone. It was a ringtone she had recently downloaded. The volume of Ruheen's phone was so loud that it normally rendered her conscious in her deepest sleeps on the most tiring nights in barely two rings, but today it took six rings to quiver her sub conscious mind and traverse her back into the present as though in a time machine, another two for her mind to liaise with her long, beautiful arms to reach for the phone and the last two rings surprisingly, to locate the accept button for she had been using that phone for over a year.

"Hello." she answered.

"Hey babe!"

"Hi Raghav."

"Heyy........, there's something about your voice today, something pleasant."

"So why wouldn't it be, Nirvaan is coming back finally."

"Yes of course," he paused, "alright so the plan is all three of you be ready in the evening, Vik and I will come over to your place and then we can go to the airport to pick him up."

"Sounds like a plan." she chortled.

And then he hung up.

Ruheen was delighted. As the evening came close, the smile widened on her face. She thought about Raghav and Vik for a change. They were her best guys after Nirvaan. She was particularly very fond of Raghav. After all others had discouraged her to wait for Nirvaan, it was along with Purnima who stood by her.

"Just follow your heart and the world will be at your feet." he had said.

She remembered telling Raghav all the time, "Nirvaan is a flirt, he'll never improve."

But it was he who always encouraged her and lifted her morale.

"All guys are flirts, big deal, they just need a nice girl like you who can satisfy all their urges. He will definitely change one day, change for himself, for you, for a better life."

There was something about Raghav's style, she thought. He had that persuasive power and the passion to inspire. And he did that with flair.

'Well, I hope he does change', she wished.

She looked at Purnima, a few benches across her. Rachna was also with her, chatting. Immediately she rushed towards them.

"Raghav called," she blushed "they are coming and then we'll go to the airport to pick Nirvaan up."

"Great," Purnima said "we'll have a get together again, should celebrate it, what say Rachna?"

"Sure, celebrate it with some booze, wow." she grew excited at the thought.

Ruheen came back to her seat, all smiles that made her look all the more beautiful. The evening, she thought, was about to come. And the airport and finally Nirvaan.

The mind is a place of thoughts that interconnect. The airport word took her back to that day when Nirvaan used it last.

"Bye Ruheen, it's getting late, I have to get to the airport."

It was the day they had met in the park behind Ansal Plaza in South Extension to bid goodbye to each other.

That was the day she saw him last.

5

COMMITMENT - *THE BIG QUESTION*

The day was hot and humid. It was the time of the year when Delhi was harsh on its people. Even in the evening the sun refused to withdraw its scorching heat. Before dipping down the horizon, it left its traces and made its presence felt.

Ruheen and Nirvaan had planned to meet in Ansal Plaza, the first mall of a modern Delhi that spanned a few acres of area in South Extension. Precisely, the lush green park that flanked the mall on the other side was the venue they had fixed. The park was very infamous for it love making rhapsodies. In every nook and corner, a couple hid behind some trees and bushes, deeply engaged, unaware and at times not bothered about the couple next to them who, themselves, were engaged in similar acts. They turned a deaf ear even to the occasional whistling of the snooping watchmen, who often located a vantage point for themselves and enjoy the merrymaking. Quite often, old lovers run into each other as the park is always densely populated with regards to its area.

Adjoining the park on the other side were beautiful ruby red coloured houses clustered together forming a stunning mosaic when viewed from a distance. The families that came for a walk from these houses were abashed by these acts initially, but later it became the most normal sight in the world.

Both had arrived on time at sharp seven , unusual, as on all previous occasions, one of them waited for at least an hour. They hugged each other followed by a little peck on the check. After having a bite from their favourite Subway, they came to the park and walked on the concrete walkway that zigzagged across it. They were holding hands.

To say theirs was a fast and unexpected romance would be an understatement. After the first kiss on their first day, both only got more attracted to each other. Ruheen had plans of marriage right after the first day she met him. But Nirvaan always resisted and behaved a bit more maturely. He urged Ruheen to be calm before making any decision and take her time. But time made her feelings only stronger, day by day. For Nirvaan however, commitment had always been a nightmare. He was never too comfortable with the idea of a serious relationship. The six months that he would be leaving for, today, would be a test of his feelings, he had thought.

Abruptly, out of nowhere, a squeal arose from Ruheen followed by little tears. "So when would you be coming back?" she spoke breaking the silence.

She had asked this question countless times, she knew the answer to it more then she knew her name.

"Six months!" she blurted answering her own question, stretching the number six excessively that made it sound like six years.

"Only six months Ruheen." Nirvaan assured her in a way that veered time.

Another silence followed.

There was something about these conversations that made Nirvaan very uneasy. It was worse than giving an oral exam. There wasn't much of a difference between a girl and an examiner infact. Perhaps, the examiner was slightly better as he never demanded a correct answer all the time.

He looked at his watch. There was still more than an hour for him to leave. The oral exam was about to begin. He felt a huge lump in his throat. He coughed.

"Do you love me?" Ruheen fired her first question. He coughed louder. *Now, that was cheating. The first question was always the easiest one. That was the rule of an exam. The examiner was definitely better, at least he would never take your case from the word go.*

Nirvaan carefully studied his options that she never gave. A 'no' would mean trouble, 'yes' a bigger trouble. Hell, what were the other options. He thought for a while. Choosing the most appropriate words, he answered "Honey, err……err……you know…., don't you?"

Ruheen smiled. She interpreted the answer. "Nirvaan I know, I know that you love me as much as I do, may be even more, then what is the problem? Why can't we take our relationship to the next level?"

"The next level…..where ?"

"Commitment, baby"

A thousand knives pierced Nirvaan's flesh. *Commitment?* That was the hardest thing in the world for him. *Why does anyone in the world get committed? There are so many better things to do. Commitment of all the things!!!* "Honey, I need more time, what's the hurry?"

"The hurry is that my parents want me to get married somewhere else, and soon."

"Hmm……………"

"You want me to get married somewhere else, don't you ?"

"N….No……No……..of course not."

"Yes, you do, I just saw a smile on your face when I said somewhere else."

"No…n…..n….o…….o….baby no…"

"You don't love me, I was wrong, you don't love me.." the tears came rolling down her cheeks. It was a thing she had expertise in. They were at her disposal. She could get them on and off as and when she felt like.

Nirvaan's horrors increased. It made him feel like puking. It was a thing he could never take comfortably – a girl crying in front of him. A few years back in school, he had broken up with a girl who could weep all day long. She was an excessively sentimental girl who spoke about giving her life for him all the time. Nirvaan decided to save his life instead and bid her goodbye.

He looked at Ruheen with eyes that demanded peace. Her weeping persisted. A few minutes later he couldn't take it any longer.

"Alright stop, please please please stop, why are you crying, I didn't even say anything."

Ruheen didn't stop.

"Alright I am sorry, very very sorry for smiling at that, please for God's sake stop crying now."

She didn't.

"Okay baby I love you, I love you from the bottom of my heart, you mean everything to me, if you could please please stop crying."

She finally did, but the tears stood right at the edge of her eyes threatening to be back like a storm warning.

Nirvaan knew he had to be meticulous in his selection of words now if he didn't want them back. He pointed towards a nearby bench and they sat. "Look Ruheen, please understand that it's been just two months since we met, we ought to give ourselves more time before even thinking of that....err...err..., what did you say....yeah...commitment."

He hated even saying that word.

Ruheen didn't say anything, she was holding on to her tears.

"I want to be sure that I'm sure before embarking on this....err.....err....relationship."

He wasn't fond of that word either.

"And when I'm sure about myself, I'm sure I'll be ready for these......err......err........things."

He looked at Ruheen who appeared confused. She lost count of the times he said *sure.*

"Continue." she ordered.

He continued very slowly, carefully picking up the right words at the right time. There was no doubt he was fond of her. The pretty face, beautiful eyes, thin black hair were all so endearing. He had never felt like that in years. But he never wanted to tie himself up all his life in the name of a relationship. He didn't want to lose her either. So telling her to wait seemed the only plausible option.

He couldn't speak for long after that. Ruheen didn't allow him to, she took control of their last few minutes together. "Alright Nirvaan, I got it, you want more time." She looked, up straight into his eyes, then asked with visible coarseness. "How much time?"

"err..........err..........about" Nirvaan fumbled. "I think these six months I'm away, would be good enough to make me sure."

"Alright so you have these six months, but you better be sure by then because I won't leave you after that."

"Sure." *At least there would be peace for the next six months now.*

The depression came back on her face. Tears were all set. "Nirvaan, I am sorry, I am so sorry, I don't want to be rude to you, but what do I do, you leave me with no other option."

"No, no its alright please don't start crying."

"You know I love you so much, more than anyone else in this world, my feelings for you are evergreen."

"Okay...." *what is she saying?*

"These feelings are an open garden and I expect a little nurturing from you."

"Sure" *Man this is sounding so damn complicated.*

"You are the gardener of this life, these feelings and love, you ought to......................"

Alright she isn't speaking English. I have to stop her now. "Ruheen I got it, I got it all." He waited for her to stop. He looked at his watch again and took a deep breath. "I must leave now, it's getting late, I have to get to the airport."

And the tears came back flowing down with brute force.

"Will you bid me goodbye with tears Ruheen, is that what you want, huh."

"No......no......no......" the tears were sucked back inside. "Nirvaan, take care of yourself."

He stood up to leave. Ruheen also got up. He kissed her on the forehead.

"You too." he said and turned around to leave.

He walked a few meters when he got a message on his cell phone. It was from Ruheen. He read it:

'They may say that distance makes the heart go fonder,

but the way I feel makes me ponder,

that even if I spend my life just looking at you,

every time I blink my eyes, I'll miss you.'

6

VIK- *THE DREAMER*

The Indra Gandhi International Airport of Delhi has evolved over the years. After the contract was signed with the GMR group of Bangalore, they have certainly risen up to the onus of metamorphosing it to a world class airport. From a squalid place thronged with people in the most disorganized way, it has been revamped as a much needed co-operative bustle.

There in the waiting lounge, lay a groggy eyed Ruheen, Vik, Raghav, Purnima and Rachna at two in the morning awaiting Nirvaan's arrival; his flight was delayed by two hours.

"So guys what about the surprise, are we still on with it." Rachna yawned.

"Yeah sure, why not." Purnima said, her resilience against sleep was inspiring.

"Guys I say let it be." Ruheen added with a tinge of concern, "he is coming back after such a long time, it's a long flight and he'll be awfully tired, and you guys plan to whack his luggage, lets limit the surprise to a warm welcome."

"Hey come on Ruheen don't you get started with that *don't trouble my baby again,* we are just having some fun." Purnima exclaimed "and" she continued with her mischievous grin "the best part is that he is not even aware that we are coming to pick him up, he'll be haunted there with his lost baggages, thieves that we are, ha ha ha ha ha ha."

Her laugh was meant to be a reprise of Gabbar Singh in *Sholay* or a yester year villain's on his way to rape the heroine, however, it ended up drawing puzzled looks on everybody's face against her midway chortle.

Purnima, of course, shut up after that.

An hour later, around three in the morning, Purnima jumped from her seat, overjoyed. "Guys, guys Nirvaan's flight has landed, get up." Everyone rose from their seats and rubbed their eyes.

An ebullient smile unleashed from Ruheen. It was a smile of complete bliss. This was it, Nirvaan had come. Her six months long wait was over. She would finally get the answer to all her questions. She was ecstatic. A slight wave of apprehension, though, still persisted in her.

"Vik you keep the car ready, meanwhile we will plan how to steal his bags from right under his nose." Raghav said. "Come on girls, time for some action."

"Yeah alright , all the best." Vik said as he pranced towards the car.

Twenty seven minutes later, Raghav was sprinting with all his brute force, Nirvaan's luggage on the trolley, being propelled with his kinetic energy. The feisty Purnima followed suit, running the fastest in her life. Her small feet, while running, covered a distance that was comparable with Raghav's but while he was walking. Still she managed to keep up in the race as the bulky Rachna trailed her by a couple of metres and Ruheen lay a distant fourth, who ran looking behind her to catch a glimpse of Nirvaan.

"H.........H.........How did you manage doing that so easily?" Purnima asked as she ran fast to keep up with him. "Nirvaan would have no clue what happened."

"Nothing much," Raghav looked behind to answer "just gave a taxi driver some money to engage him with a talk and that did the trick for me."

"Bloody scoundrel." She remarked smugly.

"Run harder" Raghav shouted, "and tell the other two behind you too."

"Hey there you are guys," Vik chortled as they came running towards him. He looked at the bags, "bloody thieves, robbing someone's bag, huh." he remarked slyly.

"Oh shut your crap up, here put it in the car." Raghav handed the trolley to him.

"Guys, some water please, I am exhausted, never ran like this before." Rachna huffed and puffed.

"Me too." Purnima boasted, "Never ran so fast, I actually felt like a real thief being chased by cops, wow, so cool no." The exultant smile on her face was incomprehensible.

A minute later, Vik howled, "Guys, where is Ruheen?"

Everyone looked around.

"Oh shit!" they yelled together as they again ran to find her.

Fifteen minutes elapsed, but their scout remained in vain. They couldn't trace her. Just then, Raghav saw something familiar, dead ahead of him. He moved forward.

As he squinted in the dark, he saw two familiar set of lips locked against each other. "Welcome to India, you asshole." he said.

"Thanks for the luggage man, I hope you kept them safely in the car." Nirvaan said.

Half an hour later, they were all at Cumesum, Nizamuddin – one of the few restaurants in Delhi that entertains the nocturnal cadre with their detectable food. At about four on a Friday morning, the place wore a deserted look mostly, with a small number of people, given that not many party on a Thursday night in Delhi. The place thus, resonated with their babbling sound.

Nirvaan remained the centre of attraction throughout the night with Ruheen cuddled along his side. They kissed often. The nitty gritty of the conversation remained his profession - merchant navy. It was a profession that demanded staying away from home for 5-6 months together on the high seas. Before this contract of his, Ruheen had thought highly about his profession. But lately, owing to the six months of separation, she changed her opinion.

As opposed to Ruheen's views, Nirvaan was proud to be a sailor. The uniform, discipline, austerity, the endless sea with no limitations fascinated him. The green dollars and sightseeing throughout the world was an addition. The pride and honour that a sailor associates with his job was unmistakably clear in his eyes when he spoke. He told them about the beautiful islands, the mountains which his ship transited, the starry nights engulfing the ocean with it long, wide mercurial arms and the serenity it possessed. The peace and tranquillity it exuded was a delightful rhapsody. A walk past the deck with the winds buffeting against the face and the occasional sprays was an experience far from satisfying. He shared his experience of traversing the Panama Canal- the one that separates North and South America, the sightseeing in the Niagara Falls, Amazon river, Rocks of Gibraltar, the Cayman Islands, Pyramids of Egypt, the nude beaches of Spain. It got all others widely interested as he spoke but the one thing that sent a chill down their spines and rose everyone on their seats was the story of pirates.

"Pirates, err...........you mean like pirates of the Caribbean?" Rachna asked first, being a passionate admirer of the movie series.

"Yes somewhat," Nirvaan replied, "the only difference being Pirates of Arabian not Caribbean."

"So what were they like?" Purnima asked, her words evinced the excitement she felt.

"Was fortunate enough not to see them, if had, then wouldn't have been here, instead would have been there sharing your stories with them."

"Wow!" Purnima drooled.

"Oh shut up Purnima, this is serious stuff." Rachna snapped. "So tell me Nirvaan what it was like."

"Well after crossing the Suez Canal of Egypt, we entered the Arabian Sea and these bastards were all there. They actually rule the Arabian Sea, and the worst is the Gulf of Aden – the area between the two countries Somalia and Yemen. Mostly these pirates are of Somalian nationality. Owing to the poverty in their country, piracy turns out to be the most viable profession. Can you guys believe that in twenty four hours, these mother fuckers hijacked 8 ships ?"

"But why the hell do they hijack ships, for money is it ?" Rachna raised an eyebrow.

"Bravo money, a whopping rupees 200 crore is what they asked of a company to release one of its ships."

"But did they get it?"

"You bet; the ship, cargo and crew are way more expensive than that."

"But what if the company refused?"

"Fireworks, they love killing people."

"But doesn't the government of these countries do anything about that?" the concern and fear together surged out of Ruheen's throat.

"Balls, these pirates roam scot free, they fire missiles and rocket propelled grenades at us, I have actually seen gun firing, the ship ahead of us got hijacked. And then like lions they boarded the ship and sailed it across to a secret location. Whether that's a secret to the government too, only God knows. And there they keep the crew hostage for months at gunpoint until the company accepts all their demands. Bloody hell, sometimes I feel as if I am in the Indian navy, gets scary at times guys."

"I thank my heavens, I am not a part of that." revelled Vik "thank God I left merchant navy way back."

"You were also in merchant navy earlier, is it?" Ruheen asked.

"Yeah, of course…I was."

"But what made you leave it?" asked Purnima, carefully tucking two strands of her hair behind her ear.

"It was not my kind of a job, useless slogging, I want to do something big." he replied, looking above as if it was there.

"And what is that big thing?" Purnima asked again, looking above at the same height as Vik had done. Perhaps the big thing was really there.

"Well guys, I'll tell you." Raghav intervened "every year my dear friend has a new dream, a new ambition which he vows to pursue, however, it always ends up in the dustbin just like an old calendar."

"Oh shut up Raghav, thats not true." Vik revolted.

"Oh really, then what about the passion you had for music once, you had said you'll be a musician one day."

"Well I realized God hadn't given me a good voice."

"Really, then cricket, what about the whole cricketer thing you wanted to be?"

"I'm an asthmatic okay, so didn't have much energy to run, hence I dropped the idea."

"and stocks, you said you wanted to rule the stock industry."

"too risky."

"Teaching, you said teaching was in your blood, professor Vik."

"I kind of developed a hatred towards studies later."

"Cooking, you had plans of being an exquisite chef too."

"Well I learnt it was more of a female thing."

"Oh.......and what about...................."

"Alright stop." Vik yelled through clenched teeth as he slammed

43

his right fist into the lacquered wicker of the table spilling his own coffee that spilled from his cup."

He gave Raghav a baleful look. Thirty seconds later he was smiling.

"Ass that you are!" Raghav threw a piece of chicken at him.

It fell on the table after hitting Vik's nose. He ate it. Everyone guffawed.

"Alright guys, laugh, laugh as much as you can, but one day I'll do something big to make you guys proud of me." he threw the bone back at Raghav. "and you too."

"One day" Raghav droned and smiled.

All this while Ruheen hadn't spoken much. She was lost in her maze of thoughts. Often, her eyes darted helplessly to Nirvaan. They had a question imbued in them, the answer to which was awaited for six months. But Nirvaan never connected to them.

Soulfully she mused to herself, *was it really worth the wait.*

7

ONE OF THESE DAYS……

"Coming, coming guys." Vik roared as he whisked through the bedroom towards the door where the bell rang.

It was Raghav and Nirvaan.

"Asshole what took you so much time." Raghav remonstrated "Its been five minutes."

"Nothing man, the usual stuff."

"Oh mom's after you again."

"Yeah," Vik's mouth puckered with dislike. "sometimes I wonder if I'm her real son, she's my biggest critic."

"No, she's the second biggest, I'm the first." Raghav laughed as they entered his house.

Vik's house was on the second floor of the DDA flats in Munirka. All the houses were pale yellow and unmistakably similar in size and shape. The entire colony was very modest in which the hard working middle class people lived. Outside Vik's house, stood a dilapidated

Maruti 800 car that his father used to drive. After his death, it was mere scrap metal lumped on four wheels.

Vik's dad had been a government official who worked in the accounts department in Punjab National Bank. He earned a paltry income connoted by the fact that he had the onus of bringing up his three children—his two daughters Manvi, Tanvi and Vik. In addition the payment of the loan he had taken only aggrawated his stricken state. He toiled day and night, supplementing his income through a second job after his work hours. Vik's mother, totally dedicated to her husband, assisted him with menial chores – stitching, ironing clothes, preparing lunch boxes and sundry. Together their income was never enough as a substantial part of their salary was spent on Vik's dad's medication, he being a heart patient. Melancholy worked through him as he fretted through his life.

One Sunday afternoon in the dining room, while being served by his wife, he collapsed right on his chair. The next moment he was dead. Heart attack was the cause, Vik's mother learnt later when the doctor arrived. She was devastated. To see her husband die in front of her almost instantly, was the single most wretched moment of her life. She could not speak for a month after that.

Owing to the responsibilities towards her children, she reconciled to her life a few months later. They became the oasis of her life. She worked very hard, their proper upbringing became her sole aim.

A few years later, came the second most happy moment of her life –the first had been given birth to her son. Vik, with his mother's blessing and hard work, got a job in the merchant navy. The high paying job, she thought, would surely end all her financial miseries.

She could get her daughters married, they had crossed that age when people raise their brow and sense something sceptical. Moreover, the loan that gnawed at her endlessly would be over. But to her dismay, Vik, in a few months left his job for reasons inexplicable to his mother.

"It was a petty job, one day I'll do something big, something different." was all he reiterated.

So his mother continued slogging, recovering from the illusion that her son would take charge of all the responsibilities. His sisters swore that marriage was a distant thought until the loan was over. But they knew for themselves, the thought would remain distant for quite a while because it was a hefty loan they worked for. In addition they had to support Vik who never thought twice before money exchanged his hands. He was the sort of person who loved splurging on credit cards and living life on credit. The thought of paying the debt never occurred to him. His mother and sisters, he knew, were there to do the needful.

Often there were quarrels between Vik and his mother who urged him to do some kind of a job and help their course. But job, he thought was never made for him, petty things like them were very ordinary and anybody could do it. He had become deaf to his mother's constant importuning and sharp criticism.

His sisters though, never criticized him for anything as opposed to their mother. Not even on the day when the marriage of his elder sister Manvi broke up due to their financial inability to organize the wedding. Vik was shattered that day and spent the entire night drinking. He pledged that soon he would get his sisters married respectfully. But a few days later, he was back to his original self, unperturbed and carefree.

Though he did try his hand at a few jobs here and there, he never really went ahead with them. His bones, like his mind had become too hollow to work. He believed someday, something would make way for him that would embark him upon this special life, of which, he had no definition. Till then he waited.

"Mom, please get us some juice and snacks, Raghav and Nirvaan are here." Vik trumpeted to his mother who worked in the kitchen.

She came out in a few minutes with a platter as ordered by Vik, shared her hellos, however with a tinge of rudeness that was perceptible even by a blind man.

"Phew, your mom is angry it seems." Nirvaan commented as she left.

"Let her be, I don't care." Vik replied, so callously that it aroused a trickle of ire in both of them.

"Vik what is it?" Raghav spoke outright, "Why can't you do a god damn job, that's all your mother wants, isn't it?"

"Or better still," Nirvaan added, "why can't you go back to the merchant navy, you'll get good money. Am I not doing it."

The ear- splitting concern through which they spoke urged Vik's mother to whisk outside with an agility that belied her age. She looked at her son with a mixture of anger and disgust.

"Oh, why would he?" she berated, "his mother and sisters are working for him day and night so that he can live lavishly, party, drink, sleep and enjoy himself. Why is he required to do a job? And where would he get a job anyway, no place starts work at two in the afternoon."

"With such difficulty," she continued, after a pause in a tone that demanded sympathy, "I managed putting him in merchant navy, but this idiot left even that. Had his father been here, he would have been stumped by his indifference and indolence."

"Look at Raghav and Nirvaan," she added regaining the rough inflection in her voice, speaking directly to Vik "are these guys not working? For heaven's sake why can't you work."

"Oh shut up mom." Vik replied rudely "Go do your work in the kitchen, how many times have I told you not to bother me with that crap of yours, I'll take up a job whenever I feel like. Besides what is the hurry."

"Yeah sure, what's the hurry!" she replied indignantly as she left the room in a huff "You are only twenty eight years old after all."

Raghav and Nirvaan started at Vik with eyes wide open. He maintained his nonchalant stance. He devoured the sandwich and glugged the juice. The stare continued.

"Alright guys, stop, let me eat." Vik said.

"I hope you realize that you are an asshole." the contempt in Raghav's voice was stark.

"Oh come on now don't you get started."

"And then some people say my mom is my biggest critic." Raghav said with great disgust. "Hell, what do you do sitting at home all day doing nothing. Why can't you take your butt outside and do some work."

"Look guys, that's not what I want to do," Vik's tone indicated his frivolous attitude, "some petty job through which I'll earn peanuts. It has to be something which I am passionate about, I enjoy doing, something like on its completion I look in the mirror and say yes Vik you did it."

"And when exactly do you plan working on that something?" Raghav pried.

"One of these days."

"Oh great," Raghav looked at Nirvaan with a faint smile and then faced back Vik, "and what is that something anyway?"

Vik thought for a while "Haven't really thought about it." he shrugged.

"So when do you plan to think about it?"

"One of these days." he replied.

8

OH GOD!!!! YOU ARE STILL NOT *SURE*.....

"Alone." she gushed, carefully tucking her hair behind her ears.

"Yes, Ruheen alone, you ought to meet him alone." Rachna declared, her husky voice resonated inside their room.

"But won't it be a better idea if……….."

"Sssshhh, alone, now do as directed."

Ruheen looked into Rachna's eyes that were a fiery red, her trademark in any discussion or debate. Immediately she disconnected from the electrifying gaze that tore through her eyes and took solace in facing the puny Purnima.

Purnima spoke without wasting a microsecond "Of course Ruheen, how can we all meet together, Nirvaan will feel so uncomfortable in putting across his feelings in front of all of us. You guys should definitely meet alone and talk it out."

"Pooh, come on you saw him yesterday, didn't you?" Ruheen cried instantly "He could not even face me directly, if I put that question today, he will feel all the more uncomfortable, better we all meet together and let him have some more time to decide."

"Yeah sure, give him another six months to decide." Rachna howled "Haven't you given him six months already, how much more time does he want?"

"Relax Rachna." Purnima tried appeasing her, offering a cigarette.

"Seriously go meet him alone Ruheen, it will be better." Purnima said.

"Alright." Ruheen capitulated.

"And another thing." Rachna yelped, "get it straight across that you want a god damn answer today, Yes or No. Stop wasting any more days of your life." She continued after a drag. "Is that clear, a Yes or No, today, tell him or else I will speak to that dickhead."

"Alright, okay, you don't need to do that." Ruheen replied. "I will be gone then."

She held her brown coloured UCB bag across her arm and disappeared through the door.

Just when she left, Rachna bellowed to Purnima. "You know what Pooh, she will never get the answer today, I know him, Nirvaan that bastard."

Barista – the coffee shop in Vasant Vihar, a two storey building is set in the bustling PVR Priya Complex. The place is dimly lit and hoops of grudging luminescence are cast by means of low power bulbs arched on the walls. Coffee sells as the place is more of a hub for conversations.

"It's been a long time," Nirvaan said, "when I was last here."

breaking the shackles of silence that had encrusted around them. It had been more than fifteen minutes and yet none of them managed to broach a conversation. It was an unmistakable contrast from their early days of acquaintance. Back then an outburst of conversation would spurt out from them like blood from a fresh wound, and relentlessly. Their confabulation with each other seemed never ending. As their friends commented wryly – they were made to talk to each other.

But today it was a completely different world. Even their eyes repelled like an innate magnet in an electromagnetic field.

'God', she thought, 'I have been waiting for this moment for the last six months to talk it out with this idiot whom I love defiantly despite all odds. Why have you made me speechless? Please give me the strength, the courage to get rid of this uncertain period of waiting right here, right now.'

Not possible, she acquiesced a moment later, for even if Nirvaan asked for more time, she would grant him. And she knew that.

Nirvaan sat motionless, with his heart in his mouth. He dreaded the lava on its way to be spewed from Ruheen's mouth. His eyes rolled sideways averting her direct gaze, tongue slunk backwards. 'God', he mused, 'how am I to answer her questions today, they have always been so difficult, six months I evaded them. Thanks to merchant navy.'

Man, I love my job!

"Err so," they spoke together, their guttural sound interspersed against each other.

Nirvaan observed Ruheen blanch noticeably. He was attuned to the nuances of her expression. It was going to come anytime now, he girded himself.

And then she spoke.

"A few months back when you left, everyone here dissuaded me to wait for you. Nirvaan would never be sure, everyone said. But I disagreed, stood my ground for I had faith in my love. But today," she paused.

Nirvaan observed a subtle hollowness crept in her voice. He felt uneasy.

"Today, I can see in your eyes, you are still not sure what you want to do with me, isn't it?"

"No, no, it's not like that. "he replied with a non-committal expression. And then he took over.

The next hour it was all him. As he spoke, like always with Ruheen, he was meticulous in his selection of words. They were carefully scouted and disgorged appropriately at the appropriate time. His eyes, with their precise movement, co-ordinated well with his rhetoric that was nothing but persuasive. It was an art he had gained perfection in, of late, but with Ruheen, he had been better than perfect.

The speech was being executed well, thanks to the many times he had rehearsed it on the ship by himself. Hard work does pay, he thought. Ruheen also contributed, but monosyllabically as opposed to her innate talent of talking easily and at length. Her soul succumbed to Nirvaan's art and she did nothing to overcome it. Rather, she just flew in like the fitful gust of wind, undulating along with it, something she had sworn invariably, she wouldn't.

The monologue continued longer than he had anticipated, but it was yielding positive results and he could see that. No more *ifs* and *buts*, no more *whys* and *whats*, no more inane comparisons and predictions, hell, no more criticism as well. And not even a single drop of tear in her eye.

'Man, I am good enough to be a lawyer,' he revelled. 'Last time it was hellish, a cut throat competition as to who would fire more.' Edified, at the thought, he continued in his best persuasive tone.

Ruheen listened patiently, bereaved at the innovative ideas that Nirvaan presented to her so that he could be *sure* that he was *sure*. One idea particularly aroused goosebumps in her, sending a shiver down her spine. "May be I should date some other girl for some time and get a little cosy with her. If a guilt factor creeps in, well then, I can be *sure* that I am one hundred percent *sure* for a ....err..........err........commitment with you, see what I mean."

Oh my god did he really say that? If I had a gun now I would have shot him dead, this very moment.

And the impassive flair with which he spoke, aroused a piercing pain together with anger in her. It felt like a hundred knives pinching and scraping her at the same time. Suppressing her fury, she proffered her most understanding expression.

He continued for another fifteen minutes, tired but never unenthusiastic. In between he paused at times to let Ruheen grapple with the situation. "And that is why I think we should give ourselves some more time to be *sure*." he concluded.

You didn't change in the last six months, did you?

"Not we," she corrected with a shade of admonishment, "you need time, I am sure."

"Oh, well...yes........I need time."

"How much more now?" she inquired impertinently as though she was bargaining with a salesman.

"Err....well...maybe.....about........I...would...say...depends, it depends."

Quoting a fixed time would mean death after the allotted time was over, Nirvaan was *sure* about that. Hence, depends.

Ruheen, however, had guessed the answer way before he spoke. She kept shut. The two months she spent with him last time, the last six months of wait, flashed in front of her. She knew she loved him more than anybody else in the world. *But why?* She didn't know.

She did not even know why she agreed to all his unjust demands. Being with him had become a prerequisite or even his feelings would suffice.

She looked at him. The sharp eyes, broody looks, chiselled features got her drooling. The ephemeral anger receded and gave way to a fondness that was ever abundant for him.

An adorable smile unleashed from her.

"Never mind," she said, "let's go."

A hundred metres away, Raghav had got a bit too enthusiastic.

"Dude, this is it, this is going to be my place, I will be the king here in the coming time." he said. He was staring at the "Jam'In pub" right ahead of him through transfixed eyes that appeared to be passionate for a dream.

Vik wasn't sure if Raghav said that to himself or to him. Nevertheless, he understood a jack. *King?*

"You think that peanut idea of yours would make you a king." he sniffed.

"Of course it will." Raghav inhaled "an invincible kind of dating."

9

THE DATING CLUB....

For the next few minutes, Raghav and Vik surveyed the place intricately. Raghav knew the Priya Complex was the perfect place for his dream. It had the perfect ambience and verve, and it bustled with just the right age group of people. He observed the crowd around him. Their average age appeared to be around twenty five.

'Perfect!', Raghav mused with a pumping rush of adrenaline that surged through his veins.

"Man, this is going to be my kingdom in the coming time, you wait and watch." he revelled.

"Yes alright Mr. King, but what about the place?" Vik asked, concerned, "Have you managed to get a hold of it".

"Sure." Raghav replied through full wide eyes that evinced his excitement. "I spoke to the landlord, the lease for this Jam'In pub is getting over in a few months' time, and then it will be all mine."

"And what about the legal formalities?"

"They will be done soon, the landlord had said."

"And for how long are you getting the lease?"

"3 years"

"Oh! hope it works for at least three years then and how much money are you paying for the initial deposit."

"He said he wants the rent for at least three months first."

"Oops, three months together, hope you have that much money."

"Of course, man, come on, I have been working for this dream like a mad dog for years now, money is not a problem, I just hope this plan works."

"The plan, yeah," Vik said, "I hope it works."

The plan was a very enthusiastic one. It had been configured after a lot of thinking, ideas and changes, besides the enormous delirium of confusion.

Raghav had been working in an investment firm for the last seven years. In the first month of his job itself, he realized that this was not what he wanted to do. The work load, deadlines, the ever sulking boss, working Saturdays and Sundays got him groping for freedom and innovation. He developed a hatred for his job that was least satisfying. It proved to be a graveyard for all his ideas and talents. He never got a chance to murture them.

Raghav was the sort of person who loved experimenting and taking his chances in life. He loved taking risks and often it worked for him, for they were always well planned risks. "Life without risks is no life at all." was his favourite one liner among his office colleagues. But his boss hated the *innovator* in him. He ordered Raghav to follow the path laid for him scrupulously. Raghav, however barely listened; life, he believed, was to create your own path and not blindly follow one.

Soon he lost interest and developed a hatred for his job as it gave no time for himself. But he restrained himself, his vision focused on the future. Often he would think. 'What work is it that I want to do to be happy?'

'Nothing!', always came the abrupt answer. True it was nothing that he wanted to do. Not that he was lazy, but he hated being bound by time. Time, he thought, should be at my disposal. I should play with it as and when I feel like. 'But how?'

Money, he knew was the answer to all his questions.

'But for money, I need to work and work meant a boss.' He developed a hatred even for that word. To him, the word BOSS was an acronym of Banishment of sleep and satisfaction. No way, he thought, can't let the threads of my life be entwined in someone else's hands and definitely not in the hands of an imbecile boss.

'But what are my other options to make money anyways? Can't be a gangster, not a drug peddler either.'

And the more he thought, the more puzzled he became. He knew earning money and fast, was not a piece of cake. But he was absolutely clear in his head. All he wanted was a big fat sum in his bank account so that the interest it would generate would enable him to live a life without work, and then he would be his own boss. He would have all the time in the world to do whatever he wanted, whenever he wanted.

The think tank that his mind was, continued wandering for new ideas. Business, he wondered one day, could be one option. 'But business of what? Clothes, food, music, cars…? Oh! just let it be.'

His uproar of confusion always ended at a bar. He would drink like a person who did not love the world he was in. A few drinks and nothing bothered him thereafter. Sooner than he realized, he developed a penchant for alcohol. A mere thought of it made him *happy, real happy.*

It was during those days of his visits at a bar in Priya complex, he met Vik. Vikram was one person who could drink anywhere and anytime. Both bonded big time. Raghav shared his idea of business with him and the enormous confusion it brought along with it. But very soon he realized, Vik was not the right person to take advice from.

Almost every evening after his office hours to get over his boss' irascibility, Raghav found himself at the bar. Coincidence or fate, he never figured out which one, but he always found Vik before him with few drinks down. And together, they gulped a few more drinks till their levels of intoxication refused anymore.

Someday during those sessions of drinking, while seated in the bar, Raghav stared continuously at his drink. "Hello, are you listening to what I am saying?" Vik yelled a fourth time. But Raghav would just not listen. Abruptly, he jumped off his chair scaring people sitting on the adjacent seat, and clambered on to the table. Vik eyed him, horrified. *Man what is he up to!*

"I got it, I got it." Raghav howled like a weird man.

"You got what?" Vik asked, stupefied.

"Here on this day, I formally declare that I will open my own pub" Raghav raised a toast standing on the table. "And that is my idea of business."

After that he collapsed, right on the floor.

The next morning he found himself in Vik's house.

"Here have some coffee," Vik offered, "you got a bit too enthusiastic last night. What about your office."

"Screw office." Raghav dismissed. "Well, I did get a bit too drunk last night, but whatever I said I did mean it."

"So you want to open a pub, huh." Vik snorted. "My dear friend do you even have an idea how much money you would be needing to open a place like that."

"I will find out." Raghav said, sipping his coffee.

"And where do you want to open this pub of yours?" Vik sniffed.

"Priya Complex."

"Dude, what is wrong with you?" Vik sniffed again, "You need to have land over there which I am sure you don't to buy land in Priya Complex, you can be sure you never can."

"Who said I am going to buy a place and then open a pub, I will take a decent place on lease or a contract like everyone else does."

"Still the rent, the initial payment and the whole set up of the place, dude you will have to pay through your rose and considering the income you earn, it's going to take you years to build a thing like that."

"5 years or 10 years, I will do it."

And then he burned the candle at both ends, working both day and right. He did overtime, worked on Saturdays and Sundays, supplemented his income by part time jobs that included on-line surveys, tuitions, writing articles. He surveyed the stock industry and invested wisely on it. The mere thought of opening his own pub enthused him with unparalleled energy and vigour, and he responded fervently. He pushed his limits and did all that a human body could endure in the twenty four hours of a day. Sleep had become a necessary evil.

The one thing that he hated the most, he did. He cut down enormously on his expenses and became miserly. He suppressed all his desires that could be fulfilled by money. Money had stopped exchanging his hands. The austerity with which he lived, he thought, would yield him positive results later.

It was during those days, he got him himself a diary. All that he wanted to do, but could not, due to time or money restrictions, he swore to himself he would do at the first possible opportunity. He wrote every little thing that thrilled him and he aspired to, in his diary. With pride and adulation, he termed his diary as "Things to do before I die." His to-do-list included activities from a dinner at Taj to a holiday in Bahamas. He segregated his to-do list into monthly, 3 monthly, yearly and 3 yearly terms. This way, he thought, he would keep a track of all his desires and made sure they were fulfilled. There wasn't any entry after 3 years, because he was sure that there was no such thing in the world that would take him more than three years to achieve. After completion of a certain task, he struck it off with a single straight line. His diary became his most prized possession.

Vik, though, always scoffed at his diary. Invariably, he found Raghav writing in it. It used to freak him out immensely. "Dude, are you going to write piss and fart timings as well." Raghav used to only smile back.

Alcohol was strictly prohibited except for Saturday nights as work began only after lunch on Sundays. Sunday was the day of on-line surveys and these days he earned good money at times only by filling forms on the net, giving his opinions about new products.

He missed alcohol immensely. His to-do list also included drinking to death every night for at least a month after his pub opened. The alcohol session that he had with Vik got transformed into coffee sessions. Coffee being a sleep inhibitor became the ultimate choice for a drink. Instantly, he developed a new found interest in coffee. It's aroma and richness of taste fascinated him.

One day while sipping coffee at Nescafe, Raghav wryly commented to Vik, "Man I could even open a coffee shop". Vik only smiled back, shaking his head in disapproval. Abruptly, yet again he jumped from his chair in a similar fashion as he did in the pub.

"Now what?" Vik grunted.

"I think I just got an idea." he replied euphoniously. "How about opening a pub cum coffee shop?"

"Balls !" Vik grunted again, "What is happening to you man?" But Raghav did not listen, he grew over excited at the thought, "A coffee shop that opens afternoon may be each day, up to say nine and then turns to a pub." "You have gone abso-fuckin-lutely nuts man."

The idea of opening a coffee place along with a pub was attributed also to the fact that since the last few weeks, Raghav was in a fix. 'What if the pub did not click. All the hard work, money in the drains.'

'No, no can't be.'

He was thinking of an alternative to the problem or perhaps an amendment. It had to be a pub, he was sure of his love for alcohol, but what more could be done got him thinking. Opening a pub cum coffee shop seemed to be a plausible idea. If the pub did not do enough business during the nights, the coffee shop would do the needful during the day and vice versa. In addition, the same place could be used for both.

The demeanour and confidence on his face got even Vik thinking. 'Man this is not entirely impossible.'

"But what about the entire ambience and set up of the place, you don't see coffee shops and pubs in the same aura, do you?" Vik inquired impatiently ruffled by the new idea.

"Right, finally a sensible one from you".

Raghav knew Vik was right. Coffee shops and pubs are not and can never be with the same ambience. Still somewhere inside him, the idea rocked. He loved being new and original. May be it's a risk, but life without risks is no life at all. He spoke after his cogitation. "Alright here is the plan – the set up of the place would be that of a coffee shop as that is during the day time, and as for the pub, a quick re-arrangement will be done at night, everyday. I will make it the darkest pub of the city, just the minimal lights would be displayed, and I truly feel that with the loud music and drinks, only a dumb ass like you is going to bother about the damn set up."

"Don't worry." Raghav added. "I will hire a good innovative designer for the place."

"Sure, all right, sounds like a plan." Vik blurted.

"And oh! you know what," Raghav boomed, "just thought of a

name for it."

Vik was all ears. "CoBo Club." He heard.

"What CoBo, what is that supposed to mean?"

"Co as in coffee, Bo as in booze, the CoBo Club".

"God you are insane." Vik castigated. "Of course not, man that sounds like some breed of a cockroach."

But Raghav was done, his mind was made, the CoBo Club was final. He grew over enthused with the thought of his new idea. It was daring to be different.

Over the next few weeks, he spent sleepless nights. So excited he became that he worked even harder to get his finances in place. *Can't wait to get close to my best life.* If everything went smoothly and at the current rate, he thought it would just be a few more years for him to establish his dreams. And then it would be all him, he would be his own boss.

There were times when Vik urged Raghav to reconsider his double game of business. "There is something so bloody unusual about a pub along with a coffee shop that it always gets me sceptical." Vik always complained.

"Dude everything in the world today was unusual when it began and over the years the very unusual became the usual, you just need the right vision to see the future." Raghav quipped.

The pub cum coffee shop idea had satisfied Raghav but still an iota of doubt persisted. *Would people actually like the concept?* He was not totally convinced. *Something surely could still be done.*

He strained his brain and did more thinking in the coming months, he was sure that he would come up with an idea, after all if he put his brain to something, it was bound to work. And he knew that. He admired this quality in him and was glad that with a little bit of planning along with proper time management, everything in the world was achievable.

Meanwhile the items in his diary kept on increasing as he hardly got time to fulfil them. But he was sure all of it would immediately be achieved after he opened his pub. Time and money would no longer be scarce then.

He made another column in his diary that read "My Daily Deeds". In it, were the items that were to be practised daily and regularly. The first item under it was to smile and be happy despite all hardships. The second was to respect the value of time. After a few weeks, he got a third item to the list. It had something to do with Vik.

The Daily Deeds column along with his diary, Raghav learnt made him more organized and prepared for life. He knew exactly what he wanted and all his energy and focus was concentrated right there. It made him all the more happy even after all work and no play. He awaited the day when it would be all play and no work.

Edified by the thought he continued slogging. He reduced his rest hours to a bare minimum. The average sleep in a day for a month never exceeded 3 hours. Yet he never felt sleepy or groggy, only more encouraged and inspired by his own hard work. After his office hours, he worked online and forayed in all money making activities. The online surveys, he learnt, earned him the maximum money.

During those days Raghav met one of Vik's friend and batch mate, Nirvaan. He was in the merchant navy and like all seafarers, desperate to get hooked. Nirvaan was the sort of person who carried his heart on his sleeve especially when his conversation hovered around girls.

"Man what a babe she is!" was his favourite one liner. He was known to have infrared eyes that could precisely measure a female's figure by one cursory look. Butt and bust were his specialty.

On occasions he got Raghav and Vik embarrassed by his lascivious glares at a woman. A flirtatious smile followed the glare that formed small depressions in the fleshy part of his cheeks. Quite often, it worked for him and then he never lost his opportunity. Raghav learnt later Nirvaan was the biggest flirt he had ever come across and a successful one at that. Still, he was never satisfied. He had a perpetual desire for women.

"Guys had I been in a college or a shore job like you, I could have scored my runs faster perhaps in fours and sixes, but to my bad luck there is hardly any social life in merchant navy." he always grumbled. Both Raghav and Vik were used to his above complaints.

One day the three of them were sipping coffee at Barista in Vasant Vihar. Raghav had managed to get some time off for himself. Vik was always off. Like always the conversation hovered around girls, women, aunties, courtesy Nirvaan. He was telling them how difficult it was for him to get in touch with girls considering his negligible social life. On most of the occasions, he was saying it was his glances and dimpled smile that did the trick. "It would be so cool," he desired, "if here in Delhi there was a dating club where people from all walks of life would be interested in meeting new people. I think that would be the best place to meet girls and then I would take it from there."

"Oh come on shut up, there can be no such thing in Delhi and even if it is there, it would never work, what say Raghav?" Vik turned towards him for the confirmation.

Raghav, however, was lost. He just got an idea from nowhere. He wore a very serious expression which changed to a relaxed one and finally a hysterical laughter tore open his face.

"Guys," he jumped again which appeared to Vik a very familiar jump. "I got an idea, a dating club" he chortled "I'll make my place a dating club also."

Both Vik and Nirvaan gave him a look of scorn and disapproval which Raghav ignored heedlessly.

"Yes guys." he continued demanding attention from both of them. "Like Nirvaan there would be so many people thinking alike, looking for a place to meet new people."

Vik and Nirvaan gave him puzzled looks.

Raghav continued. "My place is going to provide exactly that, it's going to be a bandwagon of dating, what say guys?" He finally faced them for a reply.

Both remained silent. Raghav nodded. He resumed slowly enabling them to grapple the idea. "Alright let's see, what I can do is, after the coffee time gets over it will be time for dating , say from 8 – 10 P.M and after 10.00 P.M the pub takes over. What I could do is that after 8.00 P.M only stags would be allowed, strictly no couples. All the people meet people stuff would go on and Nirvaan," he cocked his head towards him giving him a wink of pride, "if there are people like you surely by 10 nobody would be single and then of course the pub would spell its charm by offering drinks and delectable food at unprecedentedly reasonable prices."

Vik was nonplussed. He let out a sigh of scepticism. Nirvaan appeared fairly convinced. Nevertheless he remarked, "Guys I do not know if it works, but I will be the one to come every day and Raghav no entry fee for me".

"And what do you have to say Vik?" Raghav asked.

"Well considering the sex ratio of India and the mentality of Indian girls, you can be rest assured that for every one girl there would be at least 10 guys, so there would be ten gay couples for every genuine couple."

"Oh shut up that will never be the case." Raghav snapped.

"Oh no Raghav, Vik can also be wise at times." Nirvaan suggested, "Asses like me are flooded in this city, it might not work owing to the mad rush of guys."

Raghav did not want to but did think likewise. It would be a total chaos, bad for the reputation of the pub as well.

"Survey guys, let's do a survey." he spoke immediately as the idea hit him.

"What survey?" both said together.

"Let us ask say a hundred girls and if more than fifty percent appreciate it and would love being a part of it, then I will go ahead with the idea."

"And what about guys?" Vik asked.

"Idiot you think guys won't come to such a place, there would be a damn queue of girls waiting for entry, I can bet on that." Nirvaan declared.

So off they went for their survey looking for girls to ask the question "Would you like to be part of a dating club?".

Nirvaan was overexcited, never before had he approached a girl with that question. They went in three different directions and decided to meet after each had asked more than a dozen girls.

Two hours later, Raghav and Vik met at their decided location.

"So how did it go?" Raghav asked.

"Quite the unexpected," Vik said, flabbergasted, "out of the thirty girls I asked, only two said they would never come to such a place, so that makes it twenty eight out of thirty."

"Wow!" Raghav chuffed, "I asked more than three dozen females and only three of them did not appreciate the idea but all three of them were together, so I guess if I had asked them separately it would have been a different answer, never mind still more than ninety per cent agreed, see man I told you".

"Yeah great, good for us" Vik said "but where is Nirvaan?"

They spent the next fifteen minutes looking for him. They ended their search when finally they got a call from him. "Hey guys, all of them, all the girls I asked they said they would love to be part of such a place, oh and I am with one of these girls now, managed to impress her. I told her it's me who's opening this dating club, would call you guys later."

Raghav was exultant, he looked at Vik who was equally excited. It was final then, Raghav decided he would turn his coffee shop cum pub to a dating place also. Three things together meant all the less chances of a floundering business. In fact, he thought, the dating part of the club could actually become its USP.

Raghav decided to include the dating part also in his club's name. The COffee BOoze club became D'CoBo Club, D stood for dating.

"D'CoBo club, man you are weird when it come to name selection, I would suggest you do not give names to your children, you will name them Girlo and Boyo".

"Oh shut up, D'CoBo sounds chic and unusual, just like the character of the place."

A few years later, standing in front of the Jam'In pub, Raghav imagined the name of his place put up soon.

"A few months more maybe; time has come to execute my plan." Raghav enthralled, "I hope it works."

"The plan, yeah, it had better work." Vik said.

"Hey look over there, Ruheen and Nirvaan coming out of Barista, all smiles and holding hands." Vik said.

"Nirvaan must have finally accepted her, no wonder the smile on her face." Raghav said, "Damn I lost my one regular customer."

10

THE COSTLIEST BLOWJOB......

"Gosh I don't believe Nirvaan is still not ready for a damn commitment and what is more unbelievable is that you agreed to give him more time, you should have given him one tight kick his butt." The unease and anger on Purnima's face was opposed to the trademark of her sedate composure.

"So what did you expect me to do?" Ruheen exclaimed. Her voice was hollow and melancholic. "Say fuck off, you know I cannot do it, not in this life at least, I love him god damn it."

"Sure, I can understand." Purnima conceded patting her back, "But I still think you are not doing any good to yourself, I mean how long are you going to wait after all."

This was something Ruheen worried about day and night. *How long am I supposed to wait?*

The other point of concern was she had turned twenty eight recently and her family in Lucknow was pressurising her to get married.

Nirvaan was twenty six and he never wanted to get married before thirty even if he accepted her, that he had made clear to her. So even if after all the ruckus and dilemma if Nirvaan was finally sure that Ruheen was the girl he wanted to spend the rest of his life with, Ruheen had to wait for another four years at least. She would be thirty two then, and this thought was killing her slowly, day by day.

Three years back, when she was twenty five, she had bought herself a very expensive lehenga to wear for her marriage anticipating that it was in the pipeline. Little did she know then, she would have to wait more than six years for the lehenga to drape her. Dust ridden, it lay at the far corner of her wardrobe which she never even looked at.

'Four years', she mused. Ruheen knew she didn't have a bright future to talk about, not for the next four years at least. "I was happier" she spoke, in a ruffled sound that dripped with tiny droplets of regret "when I was in Lucknow. The little school that my father had started was great fun. I used to enjoy teaching those underprivileged handicapped children. Besides it was a wonderful feeling to do such noble work. It used to fill my heart with unmitigated happiness that, ever since I came to Delhi I never experienced." She paused and continued soulfully. "Sometimes I regret coming to Delhi, I was more content there."

A few years back, after being fed up of being a small town girl and mollycoddled excessively by her parents, Ruheen had decided to come to Delhi and live a life on her own terms. After a lot of protests, her parents finally conceded but not without a whole lot of advice and warnings and a bucket full of tears on her departure. It was the first time she was leaving her home to live by herself. She was twenty two years then. But for her it was bliss. The idea of staying alone and independently away from the constant curbing of her parents made her high. Besides life in Delhi was much more fast and interesting.

However, six years later, she regretted her decision. Now, even if she wanted to get back, her love for Nirvaan was stopping her. "I really want to go back now to my place, leaving all this behind."

Purnima beheld a little trickle of water leaving Ruheen's eyes. Immediately she gathered her most consoling expression. "Well Ruheen, I think it's time for you to decide what you want in life. Nirvaan has made his decision, it seems. You either give it up on him or like you said if happiness awaits you in Lucknow you could consider going back there, the distance would only help you."

Ruheen wiped her little tear away, "I think you are right, its time I put my foot down, can't be waiting like this forever."

But Purnima knew more than Ruheen that she would wait, give Nirvaan more time, may be a year.

'Poor girl', Purnima thought as she left the room.

Ruheen sat on her bed with their snap in her hand, held firmly. She stared at him with moist eyes. Her fingers ran across his face and occasionally a tear drop fell on it which she wiped scrupulously to avoid any damage to it. It was the picture of their date last year, in which she almost lost her virginity had it not been for the corrupt *thulla.*

It was a late night DevD show that Nirvaan had planned in order to reap the benefit of the darkness so as to spend some "quality time" in the shady parking lot of PVR Priya behind the heavily tinted glasses of his Honda SUV – his partner in crime in his many fucking endeavours. After the movie, the moment they stepped in the car, Ruheen could feel the heat of the burning desire in Nirvaan's lustful gaze. Her heart thumped and skipped a beat when Nirvaan placed his hand on her blue short denim skirt as he slowly glided it down to her milky white naked legs and then gradually made his way up inside her skirt. Ruheen did grab his hand, but her fragile and reluctant attempt could'nt stop the experienced Nirvaan in shoving his hands up her satin silk panty.

"Easy Nirvaan, uhh, you are getting me all wet." Ruheen groaned in pain and pleasure while Nirvaan made full use of his fingers. A passionate lip lock followed as their tongues fought with each other. Nirvaan unbuckled her skirt and yanked it downwards as Ruheen obliged submissively revealing her pink coloured silk panty. Ruheen followed suit as she undid Nirvaan's jeans who helped her cause by gleefully accepting her pursuit. Ruheen smiled at the sight of Nirvaan's hard bone swaying lecherously. "Fuck, thats big!" she exclaimed.

Nirvaan motioned her head towards his groin for a well deserved blowjob, he thought, his third in the last month. Ruheen brushed her hair and tied a good knot so as not to allow it to interfere in the task that lay ahead of her. As Ruheen's lips touched his hard flesh, Nirvaan let out a sigh of pleasure, firmly held her head and moved it up and down rather brutally, groaning relentlessly. Hardly a minute into the act, he heard a harsh noise of someone knocking against the window pane. At first he ignored it lest it spoil the fun, but later as the intensity increased, he traversed back to reality. He could vaguely notice the silhouette of a fat moustachioed man howling and commanding him to lower the glass.

Ruheen got up instantaneously pulling her skirt back up and so did Nirvaan, but it took him some more time as his jeans were way below his knees.

"oye *ladke*, what happening inside, huh?" the fat man demanded wryly.

Nirvaan's balls went in his mouth when he noticed the man wearing a khaki uniform. He hastily buckled back his jeans. "Nothing sir." he replied sheepishly.

"Come out you bastard" the *thulla* ordered. "*samajh kya rakha hai*, am I a fool?"

"No sir, no sir." he replied as he got out of his partner in crime.

"Why your chain open, huh?" the *thulla* snapped pointing towards his jeans.

"Sir because I had gone to pee, that's why."

"Where in the girl mouth, you bastard?" the cop yelled "*saala tharki log*"

"Sorry sir, very sorry, please let us go." Nirvaan let out his most persuasive tone.

"Where go?" the cop asked cunningly, "you both come to thaana now, saala doing in public place, motherfuckers."

Such a situation wasn't new to Nirvaan as he had been through them many times, still it always made him sweat profusely. He, however, knew very well to avert them. He quickly took out his wallet and flipped across the notes. He took out a hundred rupee note and handed it over to the cop. "Here sir, now please let us go."

"oye, what, you give me *rishvat*." the cop grew furious, he ran his eyes in the dark to check the note, "and that too only 100 rupees, come now I will *pakka* take you to *thaana*." he held Nirvaan's wrist firmly, "saala in the times of cigarettes you give me bidis".

Nirvaan took out a 500, then a thousand, but the cop finally conceded with two crisp thousand notes not without having a cursory look at Ruheen who sheepishly hid her face behind her hands.

"Phew!" Nirvaan thought before entering the car, *the one minute blowjob turned out to be the most expensive one of my life.*

A little smile flowed down her cheeks as she remembered those moments. "You know I love you Nirvaan then why are you doing this to me." She wiped the picture again.

"There's nothing in this world I wouldn't do to be with you. Tell me what do I do, you have made me so helpless."

She looked straight into his eyes as though anthropomorphizing the picture. She felt a heart – wrenching pain within her and her breathing grew fast and heavy.

She said nothing for the next few minutes, just stared at the picture motionlessly.

And then, she started crying.

11

THE SMELLIEST FART!!!

Rachna entered the house to find a note slid under the door-"Out for a movie, Ruheen's not feeling too well. Cheers! Pooh."

"Movie!" cried Rachna instantly, "without me, bloody fuckers."

"Oh never mind." she broke in a laughter a second later. There was a gleeful spark in her eyes that manifested the smile on her face. Her steps were short and wildly exaggerated as she hopped about the floor. She was humming the tune of a famous 'Nickelback' song. In between she shook her leg. "Hey Mishi, how's my little darling doing today." She greeted her pet and fondly poured some fish food in the bowl. The fish rose and pranced upwards. It grew wildly excited at the enthusiasm of its master and did something of a somersault on the water surface. *You look so excited Rachna, what happened?*

"I know, I know, you want to know why I am so happy today, wait I'll tell you everything from scratch." Rachna said.

It always appeared strange to everyone around Rachna about the uncanny relationship with her pet but Rachna always had the same answer. "Guys! Mishi is the best listener ever; she doesn't even blink her eyes when I talk."

Rachna took the bowl with Mishi inside it and carefully rested it on the bed and then lay next to it. She unfolded the day's events with refulgent eyes. Mishi was all ears.

Post lunch Rachna was summoned to Kazi – *the fighter's* cabin. When she entered his room, he wore an expression as if a bomb had been planted under his butt. The wiggling movement of his jet-black moustache made her all the more unsettled. Somehow, Rachna observed, it made him look even more ugly. The frown on his face was more intense, the anger far more pronounced.

'Rachna you are dead today' She mused to herself.

"Why are you staring at me like that, never saw a real man is it? Can't you see the chair? Why are you not sitting? Everything has to be spelt out to you, huh ? Bloody youngsters."

"Sir," Rachna sat quietly.

"I don't know if I have made the right decision in selecting you for this job."

"Which job sir?"

"Hell you are at least better than those other thick-headed designers in my office."

"I don't know what you are talking about sir."

"Don't interrupt me, I'll tell you what I mean."

"Yes sir." She listened patiently.

"Alright the deal is as you know that India Fashion Week for November 11 is round the corner to showcase the Fall Winter 2011 highlighted collection."

"Right Sir."

"So after a lot of rumination, I have finally decided that your contemporary collection would be the highlight on the ramp for our Fall Winter 2011 range."

What? Did he really say that. Rachna pinched herself. No it wasn't a dream. Then another pinch. Definitely not a dream. *Oh my God that's real.*

Rachna knew she just got the biggest opportunity of her life. Getting to showcase her collection on such a big platform for any new designer was always a far-fetched dream. If her work was appreciated that would be the first step towards her dream of being a reputed fashion designer of India. This was a dream she had been living with right from her school days, the passion of which eventuated her admission in Pearl – the fashion designing institute in West Delhi. She did a three and a half year course in Fashion designing and obtained a degree in Fashion Designing and Technology. A month later, through campus placement she got a job with 'Silhouettes and Styles', SnS. Her happiness had known no bounds then. Today she was far more happy.

Rachna knew there would be a horde of international buyers present for the event having an access to the stalls of SnS together with the stalls of other renowned and acclaimed designers of the country. And the stall of SnS would include Rachna's contemporary designs. So she reckoned, if her designs were admired, she would have her share of contacts of international buyers. And then her dream of being a reputed fashion designer would appear much, closer and more realistic.

"What happened?" the fighter clicked, "Are you with me?"

"Yes sir, of course," a smile lit up her face.

"Alright so what I want you to do is select thirteen best styles from your collection for the season apt for the show. Make sure you do the right selection."

"Yes sir."

"And I give you the complete responsibility of the selection of your designs, matching accessories, model fittings and also coordination with the event management team."

"Right sir."

"Mind you, I don't want any goof-ups, is that clear? We must do a good job."

We must do a good job? "Sure sir, *we* will."

Rachna knew whenever Kazi said "we must do a good job, it always meant *you* have to do a good job. There were some other trademark Kazi statements which Rachna particularly was very good at translating.

"You have done a great job" meant "More work to be given to you."

"We must find out the real reason" meant "I'll tell you where you fault is."

"I am very open to new ideas" meant "I'll decide what is to be done" and then of course there was this ominous "All the best" that always meant "You are in trouble."

Rachna thanked Kazi and stood up to leave.

"Oh and maybe with that extra work and effort, your paunch would go in by a few centimetres, ha ha ha." Kazi laughed at his own joke. It strained his cheek muscles. It felt different, the last time he got that feeling was two weeks back. Rachna, however, remained silent. She did not move or smile, just stared at Kazi with blazing eyes. *Very funny, bloody asshole.* Kazi stopped laughing at Rachna's irreverence to his joke. He did not appreciate it. You have to always laugh at Kazi's jokes. The frown returned. The anger returned.

"Okay, okay get out now and *all the best.*"

I am in trouble. Rachna turned around to leave. Just before opening the door she did something that she specialized in.

The stench left Kazi with his handkerchief pressed firmly to his nose for the next fifteen minutes until rescue operations arrived in the form of an air freshner that was superfluously sprayed in the room. *Damn you Rachna!*

When she came out from his cabin, Rachna fell euphoric and was beaming with gratification. The world outside Kazi's cabin appeared to be a different place or perhaps she felt that she was not the same person. The idea of her designs being showcased in India Fashion Week 11 had overjoyed her. Now, she swore, she would make full use of this opportunity. The thirteen designs that she would choose would be the best from her collection. In fact, she wondered, if something more could be done to enhance their quality. *Let's see what I can do.* She knew she had a task at her hand and she would not leave any stone unturned to achieve her dream. This, was of course the first step.

She came towards Ruheen's desk. Purnima was also there sporting her new hairstyle. She was taking Ruheen's opinion on how it looked.

"Hey people, do you even know what just happened?" Rachna asked. Her face blossomed with excitement.

"You must have got a new boyfriend, what else?" Purnima replied, irritated that Rachna interjected her *hairy* conversation.

"No, of course not, *the fighter* just told me my contemporary designs would be showcased at India Fashion Week 11. Guys do you even know what that means!"

"Oh my God, really," Ruheen chuckled, "that's wonderful."

"Isn't it?"

"Wow Rachna that's great, I am so happy for you." Purnima said.

"Thanks, now you guys see I'll make sure my designs are liked by one and all."

"And if you are able to impress any international buyer, that will do wonders for you." Purnima said.

"Of course it will, I can start my own work then or may be can work as a freelancer together with my office." Rachna salivated.

"Great, I wish you all the best Rachna, do well."

"I will." Rachna winked "Alright people I'll see you later, going out for a smoke."

Mishi was over excited. It was fluttering her fins all over the water. In between she reprised her acts of leaping through the water from the bottom of the bowl to the top.

"I know, I know you are elated Mishi, so am I" Rachna said lying on her bed facing her pet directly. "And you know what Mishi, that asshole of a designer Zibby was so damn jealous of me, he couldn't even face me for the entire evening. Well, I guess that's the prize he paid of being my competitor in office."

"Anyway," she continued, "now you see I'll work very hard and fulfil my dream of being a successful fashion designer."

Mishi fluttered her fins again. As per Rachna that was the sign of best of luck.

"Thanks, Mishi thanks for all the support, I think it's time I get a drink for myself." She got up from her bed and left the room to get her evening booze.

Mishi was still fluttering her fins. She finally settled at the bottom of the bowl and winked. *All the best my darling*

12

"WALK IN SINGLE, WALK OUT COUPLE"

Raghav was never too fond of coming over to Vik's house. Nothing to do with the size or appearance of it, in fact, he loved the simplicity and serenity of his colony in Munirka. It was something about the aura of his place that made Raghav queasy. His unease was further accentuated by the fact that Vik was invariably discourteous towards his mother and sisters despite their humble effort to run the house without his help. It was always a deplorable sight of them getting insulted by Vik who seldom paid any attention to them.

Raghav, however, tried relentlessly to make Vik improve his attitude towards life or at least towards his family, but it was always in vain.

"Raghav please, I don't know what their problem is, they always want me to work. I don't understand what is the damn hurry, I have all the time in the world to work, besides that's not what I want to do in my life. It has to be something that I love doing, but these people, they never understand."

In spite of Raghav's arduous efforts, Vik's statement never changed. Neither did his insolence towards them.

On a bright Sunday afternoon after Vik's constant importunings, Raghav finally agreed to visit his house, but as always he felt a bit uncomfortable. Vik's mother was in the kitchen preparing lunch. His sisters were home too and in their room. Raghav and Vik sat in the drawing room. Vik's mother got them coffee and snacks. She greeted and was back in the kitchen.

Despite his discomfort, Raghav appeared excited about life. It was evident from his eyes that radiated vivacity "You know Vik," he began, "it's been almost seven years now since I decided to open my dating club and now it's just about three months for my dream to be a reality."

"Yeah I know, that's great."

"But you know what, I am still keeping my fingers crossed. Though I love my idea because of its novelty, it does get me sweating at times."

"Sweating, why is that?"

"I mean the other day I was just thinking how I would manage the timings of my place, think about it practically. I can't be on the spot with my timings. I had planned that by 8 pm it would be time for dating, but how would I achieve it, can't just chuck out people at 8 who are still sipping their coffee."

"Hmm right." Vik thought. He lit a cigarette. "Or may be what you could do is keep your last order of coffee till say half past seven."

"So?"

"I mean that's a polite way of saying: guys get out of my place by 8."

"Ha ha ha," Raghav smiled, "yeah I can actually do that." Raghav paused to visualize the scene. "And perhaps initially there could be a bit of chaos, but later when people know about the character of the place, they'll automatically get used to the timings, I mean this happens everywhere, you just have to get used to something."

"Yeah true, I am sure it will be okay."

Raghav pondered for a few minutes. Vik continued smoking.

"Alright tell me something," Raghav paused. He continued when his eyes lit up, "if today there is a group of guys without girls craving for enjoyment they just have to satisfy themselves with alcohol and music in a pub but after my place opens they can do that together with some blind dates as well."

"Yeah of course, any guy would love coming to such a place."

"Alright let's take our case." Raghav jumped with excitement. "If I, you and Nirvaan were to choose spending a boy's night out somewhere, we would obviously prefer a dating club over any other ordinary pub, isn't it?"

"Of course, who would want to go to a damn pub and just sit and drink, everybody would prefer a place where there are girls who are single and ready to mingle."

"Sure, and I think the girls would also think likewise; they are not behind us in any field after all."

"Right, our survey had proved that, I remember asking a group of girls that day and they appeared exhilarated at the thought. One of them actually said 'wow that means I can get a new date for myself every day.'"

"Of course why not! you can come every day, I won't restrict the entry for anybody, all except couples are welcome, couples of course after 10 pm, I don't want to overcrowd the place unnecessarily. From 8-10 pm the atmosphere inside the club should be that of singleton, everyone should get a partner for themselves, that's how the place would become exciting and a success."

"Sounds okay to me, however everything said and done, don't you think you are being a bit unfair to couples, denying them entry before ten."

Raghav contemplated "you think so?"

"I don't know, maybe."

"See they are most welcome after ten, but if they want to come before that they can do so by coming separately at different times, perhaps if they are bored with each other and want to seek a new date."

"Then you can call your place a break – up club, ha ha ha."

"Not funny," Raghav condemned "thinking about couples coming at different times, may be people like Nirvaan could think about that."

"Yeah." Both smiled. *Nirvaan that asshole.*

"He can never get enough girls in his life, never a satisfied soul," Raghav commented lightly, "God help Ruheen."

Vik nodded. "Anyway" he exclaimed "I don't know about girls but I am sure every guy in this city would be in love with you if this club works."

Raghav wondered about that. It was a brilliant feeling of his dream getting close. It had been more than half a dozen years when he first thought about it. Now it was less than three months. His feelings were a blend of excitement, apprehension and jitteriness. But there was something inside him but that made him confident that he would succeed. Success, he knew, was not all about winning, but giving your ambition a try. And he was doing just that.

"Raghav, please don't mind but just a thought, I know it's a good idea, but what if this dating part doesn't work."

Raghav nodded, "Well if it doesn't work, I don't see it as much of a problem. I would just limit my place to a coffee shop cum pub then, that's the beauty of my idea, CoBo would prevail."

"Yeah right," Vik agreed "or may be it works because of it's unusual character."

"Oh just let it be." Raghav dismissed, "Don't think too hard, I have done my best, rest is all fate."

"Of course."

"Anyways chuck that. Did I tell you about the punch line that I have decided to promote my club?"

"No, what is it?"

"WALK IN SINGLE, WALK OUT COUPLE."

"Hey hey hey, that's great, I like it, that will surely do a great job of exciting people especially guys"

"I hope so, I am so much looking forward to it, can't wait for these three months to get over, I feel so damn inpatient now."

Vik could see Raghav's words evinced the excitement he felt. There was a lot of energy he radiated. He knew his friend was full of life and completely on top of it. Somehow even he felt a part of his dream. He too desired it to be a success. That was the least, he knew, he could have done.

"And" Raghav continued "I have also approached a local hoarder to post the hoardings of my place along with the punch line at all the strategic locations across Delhi including all the PVRs, after all that's where the young crowd hangs out."

"Yeah that's nice, I am sure that will do the important task of luring youngsters to our club." Vik spoke scratching his head. "I mean if I was to come across such a hoarding, I would have made sure I visit the place at least once."

"Isn't it?" the pupils of Raghav's eyes dilated, "And anyone who comes once is bound to get addicted to it. I'll make sure I'll restrict the price of food and alcohol to a bare minimum. I want people to love the place first, get used to it, then I'll think about my business."

"Sure it makes sense" Vik replied "And I must say I really like that punch line of yours , it could do wonders I think."

"Definitely," Raghav replied, "and in addition I have this school friend of mine who is a Radio Jockey with 104 FM. I have approached him and his boss and they have agreed to promote D'CoBo club on the radio."

"Wow thats fantastic."

"Yeah, they said in a week's time the advertisements of my club would be on air and that will go on throughout the day, right till the time the club opens. That will surely do the imperative job of spreading awareness amongst the youth, what do you say?"

"Certainly." Vik replied. He looked at Raghav with admiration. "Dude I must say you are one person who is hell bent on achieving his dream. I mean you are so damn prepared for it, it's still about three months to go, but everything looks set already."

"Of course Vik, you know me. I don't want to take any chances with life, life is really short, you never know what's in store for you tomorrow."

"Yeah right." Vik nodded.

"And that's why I tell you all the time wake up, go pursue you dream of doing something big, success won't come walking towards your door, you have to make a move, and fast because life is short, really short, you have to be on your toes if you want to achieve something in life."

"Alright Raghav, not again please, I'll do what I have to one day."

"Damn your one day." Raghav condemned as he stood up, "I hope your one day does come someday, anyway excuse me, I am off to the loo."

Raghav had his club dream wherever he went to. Even inside the loo, he closed his eyes and visualized his club getting set up soon. It brought a smile on his face and a sense of achievement together with satisfaction. "Damn these three months!" he uttered to himself.

Vik's sisters' room was adjoining the washroom. When Raghav came out of the loo, he heard Manvi confabulating with Tanvi in a tone that appeared hollow and melancholic. Raghav didn't want to but found himself glued to their conversation. It was about Manvi's marriage.

"Manvi, I don't know if what you are doing is right, I mean how can you refuse such a wonderful proposal. Karan is a nice guy, I'm sure he will keep you very happy."

"Yeah I know," Manvi replied in despair, "but I can't be so selfish and leave this house for my own happiness, what about you, mom and that hefty loan we have to repay. I don't expect Vik to do anything, he's useless."

"You don't worry about that, I'll take care of mom and as for the loan, I'll repay it slowly with my job, you should just think about marriage."

"No Tanvi, of course not." Manvi replied in disaccord. "I can't marry till the time at least Vik realizes his responsibilities. Besides where is the money for marriage, whatever we earn goes for that damn loan."

Tanvi knew her elder sister was right, money was always their problem. "Damn" she said "I can't believe that you can't get married because we don't have money and damn this Vik, I hope nobody gets a brother like him."

Raghav couldn't take that anymore. He came out from there and went straight towards the hall where Vik sat. Vik was busy smoking. Raghav tried appearing normal. "So Vik" he spoke casually "when are you getting your sisters married?"

"Getting my sisters married," Vik started laughing, "you must be joking, how can I get them married, I am not even working."

"So how do you plan their marriage then?"

"Plan, marriage what are you talking about Raghav?" Vik replied puzzled "I don't know, never even thought about it. How can they get married anyway, you know we don't have any money? Maybe later."

Raghav couldn't suppress his anger anymore. He erupted like a volcano. "You asshole when will you grow up and learn to take responsibilities. Manvi is thirty one, do you even know she is not getting married due to financial constraints and for a brother like you."

Vik remained calm. He let out a sigh. *Not again Raghav.* "So what do you want me to do?" he inquired impertinently.

"You jerk, at least have some shame." Raghav remonstrated "Go and do some work and assist your sisters."

"And what will happen if I work?" Vik replied "She wouldn't be able to get married anyway, there's a damn loan on us."

"So does that give you an excuse not to work," Raghav castigated, "huh! is that so."

Vik didn't reply. He turned his gaze away from Raghav and sipped his coffee.

"You moron, you treat life as shit, just dump and flush, one day you'll learn a lesson for sure and it would be a very expensive one."

"Alright Raghav please." Vik exclaimed "Stop it man, why do you have to criticize me all the time."

Raghav didn't answer. He shook his head in disgust. "Look Vik, I don't know about you, but I am going to get Manvi married."

"What?" Vik stared in bewilderment "What are you saying, you don't have money either."

"I do have." Raghav claimed fatuously. "I'm not a jerk like you. I have saved enough money for my club, I can manage to take out some from there. Manvi's marriage is equally important, besides it would hardly cause a delay of a month or so. Can take that for Manvi anytime."

Vik's expression changed. He never expected that sort of a gratitude from Raghav. Though he knew Raghav would have done anything for him, but so effortlessly and quixotically was indeed a revelation for him. Something inside him flinched. He felt a huge lump in his throat. He didn't speak for the next few minutes. Neither could he look into Raghav's eyes.

"What?" Raghav asked stunned by his silence.

"Raghav, you serious?" Vik asked ruffled by his generosity.

"You know me Vik, when I say something I mean it."

Vik went quiet again.

"Alright stop wasting time, get up and let's go to my place, I'll give you a cheque."

"Now?" Vik asked in curiosity, "I'll take it tomorrow, what's the hurry."

This idiot. "Alright Vik listen, if you can do something today, do it today, if you can do something now, do it now."

Vik didn't utter a word thereafter. He was beckoned by Raghav towards the door as they left the house moments later.

"Oh my God, is this real!" Vik was swamped by Raghav's favour. He eyed the ten lakh rupee cheque presented to him as casually as a ten rupee note. His eyes grew wide, the size of a football. They fluctuated between "PAY VIKRAM OBEROI" and "TEN LAKHS ONLY". It took him a few minutes to grapple the situation and learn that this, truly, was not a dream. The moment, the cheque and Raghav in front of him were all true. He looked at Raghav with moist eyes and a feeling of admiration and gratitude for him.

"Raghav but tell me something, how can I take this money from you, you have worked so hard for it."

"Come on Vik," Raghav replied, "what use is my hard work if it cannot make me help my best friend."

"But what about your club?" Vik cried "Won't that get delayed."

"No of course not, I have saved enough money for that, don't worry, I'll take care of it."

Vik nodded. He remained silent for a few minutes. He looked at the cheque again. It was definite the money was sufficient to get Manvi married. Vik was elated that at least once he would be able to spread some happiness at home. His mother would be far from pleased. He turned up to face Raghav again.

"Thanks Raghav. I must have done some great deeds to have a friend like you."

"And I must have done some killer sins that means." Raghav smiled. "Ha ha." he laughed at his own joke patting Vik's back.

"Never mind Vik, but I sincerely hope that you start taking your life seriously and learn the importance of time. Life is beautiful, you have to live it to enjoy it, but as of new you are not living it, merely spending it."

Vik shook his head silently. He couldn't quite relate to what Raghav said but still nodded piously.

"And have you decided about that big thing you dream about doing one day."

"No," Vik replied sheepishly, "haven't really got the time to think about it."

"Time, you don't have the time." Raghav sneered, shaking his head in disbelief. "You must be joking, no one in the world would have more time than you Vik."

"Alright please Raghav, not now, I am in the least mood for a lecture."

"Okay okay." Raghav conceded, "I think you should get back home now and please take care of the cheque."

"Yup." Vik stood up to leave.

"Hey just wait Vik," Raghav called, "what are you going to say at home? Where did you get that much money from?"

"You gave it, of course, what else?"

"No no, don't say that, Manvi will never marry, she knows I have worked like crazy to earn that money."

"So what else do you want me to say?"

"Let see err.... err....." Raghav pondered. He could not think of anything.

"There is nothing else I can say, Raghav come on let it be. I'll just say you gave it to me."

"No no don't say that." He surveyed his options, again. His eyes fell on a newspaper which had some article lottery in it. "Lottery" he yelled immediately when he saw it. "Tell your mother you have been putting your money wisely in a lottery and after years you finally won one. They would be thrilled really."

"Yeah" Vik contemplated "I can do that."

"In fact when you tell them you had been putting all the money that they have been giving you on a lottery and not elsewhere, they would be delighted. The hatred they have for you for being a spendthrift would recede. See what I mean, it will benefit you both ways."

"Right, thanks." Vik's expression grew solemn. "Raghav how am I ever going to repay you this."

Raghav smiled in a childlike way, "Just make sure you do that big thing you hoard of doing one day so that you make your family, myself and our friends proud."

Vik looked at Raghav and winked "Of course I will."

13

'THINGS TO DO BEFORE I DIE'

The next month, the six of them decided to meet for dinner. It had been quite a while since their last get together considering their busy schedule owing to work pressure. Except Vik of course who had been busy only daydreaming. Their last rendezvous was at Manvi's marriage.

As is always the case, the guys were on time. The meeting point had been Big Chill Restaurant in Kailash Colony Market. Owing to its wide range of food and drinks at affordable prices, it was the best place for dinner. Raghav had suggested the place, "A few more days," he had formally announced , "then it will be food and drinks only at D'CoBo Club."

At Big Chill, they booked a table for six and ordered some snacks.

"So Vik," Nirvaan began, "I must say that I really appreciate that you got your sister married".

"Thanks," Vik replied hesitantly.

"We people really enjoyed ourselves that day, isn't it Raghav?"

"Of course." Raghav replied, "It's always good to be around with all your friends."

Nirvaan nodded. "But Vik tell me something, how did you manage the financial part of it, I mean you don't even work."

Vik remained silent. He didn't have an answer to that. He looked at Raghav.

"Lottery," Raghav answered immediately before Vik could say anything. "He had put his money in a lottery."

"Lottery, wow," Nirvaan howled, "I wish I could win a lottery like that. But which lottery did you put your money in Vik?"

Vik had no idea what to say. He again looked at Raghav.

"The Charming Prince Lottery." Raghav replied hurriedly. He thought a second later that he could have done better than that. Vik also got bamboozled at the name. *The Charming Prince..... What? I could have definitely got a better name than that. Damn you Raghav, you are always bad at names.*

"The Charming Prince Lottery?" Nirvaan thought hard, than commented sheepishly. "I think I have heard that name before."

Raghav and Vik looked at each other and smiled. *Yeah right.*

"Anyway I think its going to be some time before the girls come, so why don't we guys take a short nap."

Raghav and Vik laughed. They knew Nirvaan was right at least this time, because he had the experience. Ruheen was very popular for never being on time owing to her last minute make-up and hair style. She had acquired this quality from Purnima. Purnima was an extremist who never believed in being on time. "Let the guys wait, after all they are made to wait for us." was her explanation.

Ruheen, however was slightly better. Initially, she had often made Nirvaan wait only for an hour, an hour Nirvaan had learnt later was on his good days.

Nirvaan's idea of a nap today wasn't exactly a bad idea. A few kilometres away in Defence Colony, a whole new pandemonium had started in E-46. The great minds of the girls were engaged, a big decision had to be made. A meeting was called with the agenda: "What clothes do we wear today?"

"A halter neck would be a bad idea considering we are not going to for a disc".

"Spaghetti? No, not a good idea either."

"Something traditional? Nah, doesn't suit the occasion."

"Something casual? A jeans and a top should suffice I guess, what do you say?"

"Yeah that should be alright, but which colour?"

"Good question, let me think, what day is it today?"

After clothes, there were other important issues to be discussed like hair: open, plaited, straight, ponytail. Footwear: sandals, stilettos, wedges, pumps, shoes. Accessories: belt, bracelets, watch, bag (white, black, leather, small, big). And of course, last but never the least the face: kajal, mascara, blush on, eye shadow, lip stick. Purnima – the sartorial genius, also spent time thinking on the type of bra to be worn to suit the occasion – halter, strapless, cross back or the normal.

The meeting was finally over after a few minutes of survey of themselves in the mirror. *Good job done.* They congratulated each other. *Time to leave.* "What time is it?" Purnima asked, eyes stuck in the mirror. *Not that it mattered.*

There at Big Chill, Nirvaan put forth his true feelings regarding Ruheen after Raghav's and Vik's constant importunings.

"Of course I like her, but I am not sure if she's the one to get married to."

"Then what are you sure about." Raghav pried.

Nirvaan thought for a moment. "Ah well, actually nothing." He shook his head, then continued "look guys I don't know how you would react to it but the fact is that I am not ready for a commitment or maybe afraid of it or maybe uncomfortable about it or maybe all of them, see what I mean."

"Besides," he continued with a deserted look on his face, "I can't relish the fact that after I get committed, its going to be only her for the rest of my life, guys imagine." The deserted look was on the verge of shedding tears. "Just one girl for the rest of my life, can you believe that."

Sure we can, you think we have never thought about a damn commitment.

"I mean come on," he continued "I can't do that to myself, there are so many pretty girls out there, I'll miss them so much," he spoke with a sad look as if life had stripped him of everything he ever had. "this whole commitment thing makes me feel all the more lonely, guys imagine all the flirting, the first date, first hug, first kiss all gone, I can't be so mean to myself, don't you think I am right."

Of course you are.

"And the most important part," the deserted look gave way to a haunted one. "do you guys have any idea how much a female soul can trouble a male. Ruheen is just my girlfriend minus commitment, still she makes me shiver, so many complaints and objections – no phone calls, no messages, you don't ever love me anymore, you have changed so much, long distance relationship is all about communication, blah, blah and more blah, just imagine if I am in a commitment with her what would she do to me, everyday I would feel like a damn prisoner."

"And" he continued with his terrified look, "you know that......."

"Alright stop." Raghav and Vik yelled together. "Stop it man. Why the hell are you scaring us?"

"Guys this is one hundred percent true, I am not scaring you, I know girls much more than you guys."

"Okay, Okay, stop it now."

They ordered two glasses of cold water, one for each of them. The next five minutes they were quiet, looking around them. Surely the girls were all over the guys. The poor guy on their adjacent seat couldn't even have the drink of his choice. Thanks to his lovely girlfriend. Slowly they tried to absorb the truth.

"All said and done Nirvaan, the fact of the matter is that you have to get committed some day or the other, then why not with the girl you like." Raghav said which he thought was a wise statement.

"Yeah alright, I feel that Ruheen is good, really good, but maybe I'll get a better girl tomorrow."

"And what if you don't?"

"So big deal, Ruheen is there anyway."

What a prick!, Raghav thought about Ruheen. Her charming face, adorable personality, transparent nature was a complete mismatch to

Nirvaan's character. *Lucky bastard.*

"You won't get a better girl than her, trust me." he declared.

"Alright we'll see."

"You know Nirvaan," Raghav said, " you are like that person who enters a garden full of roses, but not satisfied with the rose keeps on moving ahead in anticipation of the best rose, till he reaches the dead end and then there's no looking back."

"Nice thought Raghav, but isn't it everyone's birth right to desire for the best." Nirvaan replied.

"Sure it is, but it is the same desire that dumps us in the drain of sadness. Don't wait for the best, whatever you have make that the best, our search for best will never get over but life will, besides Ruheen is such a wonderful person, getting her love is better than the best."

Nirvaan thought about her. Her soft hair that settled carelessly over her aesthetic ears, her flushed complexion, the deep eyes. *Sure she was pretty and worth it. But may be some more time.* "I'll think about it." he chirped.

"Sure do, think, but not like this asshole sitting right here, he also has been thinking for the last few years about doing something in life, but he's still thinking."

"Oh shut up Raghav." Vik retaliated, "I'll do it one of these days."

"Oh you mean none of these days, don't you? Anyway I do hope that you at least get started in a decade or so."

"I will man, I will." Vik replied.

A few more discussions, advice and criticism and the girls arrived. They had been very decent in being only an hour late. The guys had certainly not expected them so early.

"Hey guys, hope you didn't wait for us too long." Purnima's statement was a motley of humour and concern totally mismatched with each other. The expression, however said it all – "As though we care."

"No of course not." Raghav said, "In fact you came earlier than we had expected."

"Great!" Purnima said grabbing a seat that offered her a panoramic view of the mirror towards her side.

They ordered some food and drinks as they settled down.

"So Raghav what's the status of your D'CoBo Club?" Purnima asked as her eyes darted in and out of the mirror.

"A little more than a month maybe." Raghav replied allowing himself a smile of pride.

"Wow that's great." Rachna said as she grew anxious, "I hope the entry would be free for us at least."

"Sure it's your place, feel at home."

"Thanks and I'm really looking forward to the dating part, I wonder how that will unfold." Rachna said excitedly.

"I'm keeping my fingers crossed for that." Raghav replied, "Though I feel it will either be a huge success or straight in the dumps, it can't be anything in between."

"Don't you worry about that brother." Nirvaan announced, "It will definitely be a success, I'll come everyday and attract the girls like a magnet."

Ruheen turned to face him. She stared at Nirvaan with blazing eyes and a scowl that said it all. 'What did you just say? Try saying that again.'

"No, No," Nirvaan replied, terrified, "I don't mean I'll attract them, I meant the character of the place will attract the girls like a magnet."

Better. "Why do you have to even bother about the dating part Nirvaan." Ruheen asked in a pesky voice "don't you think you should mind your own business."

"Yah….err…..right……err……of course."

"Alright guys, please don't get started with a squabble again." Purnima quipped, eyes focused on the mirror. *This strand of hair is not where it should be, let me see what I can do about it.*

This was not a very uncommon trait of Purnima. Often she would forget the conversation around her and get engrossed in the mirror. Sometimes it was a single hair that was out of place and sometimes the entire bunch. As enthusiastic as a bee, she was always upto the challenge. After her work, she would turn back to participate in the conversation, but with the mirror around, she could hardly concentrate.

Nirvaan was observing her and getting agitated all this while. *What the hell is she doing? Who's even looking at her damn hair?* He tried moving his gaze away from her. But he could hardly control himself. The next time he caught her. "Oh God, the mirror again!" he castigated, "Pooh are you a narcissist by any chance?"

"Nar-cis-…. what, first tell me what that means, then I'll tell you if I'm one."

"Well," Nirvaan tried explaining, "A narcissist is a person who is excessively interested in himself and his physical appearance. The word is derived from Narcissus, a beautiful youth in Greek Mythology who fell in love with his reflection."

"Vo Vo Vo, Mr. Words knows yet another word, three claps for him everybody." Rachna announced with in a snobbish grin.

"Stop calling me that," Nirvaan protested "have you forgotten the day of 100 words, when I crunched you to death with my extraordinary vocabulary."

"Yeah, Whatever."

A few months earlier, Nirvaan, Ruheen and Rachna were sitting in the amphitheatre of Ansal Plaza. It had been more than two hours together and they got fed up with their own nonsense blathering, so they started passing their time by merely observing other people.

"Hey look at that guy, he's so damn scrawny." Rachna stated. Nirvaan nodded with a faint interest.

"Oh I am sure you would know what scrawny means." Rachna snubbed.

"Who me?" Nirvaan replied scornfully. "Don't you mess with my vocabulary."

"Oh really!"

"I'll kick your ass on that, I'll ask you 100 words right now and you won't be able to tell the meaning of a single one."

"Go ahead." Rachna ordered.

And so the bet began, one by one both fired words at each other. Ruheen played the judge and ensured the bet proceeded smoothly and fairly. To Rachna's dismay, Nirvaan was right. She was unable to give the meaning of any of his word correctly. Nirvaan on the other knew all her words. Stupefied, she excused herself to the loo. There she called up her friends for help. Within a minute she got a horde of words on her cell. With pride and dignity she returned and fired them at Nirvaan. Little did Rachna know, that he actually had a breathtaking vocabulary. He answered all of them with unmistakable ease.

"You must be preparing for MBA." Rachna exploded, " No wonder you know all the words, no big deal."

Nirvaan and Ruheen couldn't stop themselves from a wide-mouthed laugh.

Since that day Rachna went ballistic whenever she heard a word from Nirvaan that she didn't know the meaning of.

"Oh I wish I was there on the day of 100 words, it would have been sure fun." Purnima desired earnestly.

Nirvaan went close to Rachna, looked dead straight in her eyes and spoke contemptuously. "Yeah you would have roistered in the cascade of my tempestuous act that day."

"Whatever that means!" Purnima said disinterestedly.

"Guys excuse me, I need to call." Rachna said as she walked off.

"Guys did you see that!" Nirvaan exclaimed, "she would have killed me if she had a gun. Boy I love that sullen look on her face."

Everyone laughed. Purnima as well with her gaze in the mirror. *Hair is fine, face is fine, just need to work on my facial expression while laughing.*

Half an hour later, Rachna returned, self-possessed and calm. Ruheen could still see a shade of unease on her face. "So Rachna," she began to comfort her, "how's the work going for the fashion show?"

"Yeah, it's all set, just about a weak to go. I'm looking forward to it."

"Looks like you are totally upto it."

"Absolutely. This is my one chance to prove my worth. I won't lose it, whatever it takes."

"Great, I like your determination, I'm sure you'll be successful, what do you say Nirvaan?"

"Yeah of course." Nirvaan replied, "She has all the necessary talent in her except for vocabulary."

Rachna gave him a don't – you - dare - get - started - again look.

"Alright guys peace, I've got something interesting to tell you all." Raghav intervened in an ever excited tone of his "By the next month and by God's grace D'CoBo Club will be all set in the PVR Priya Complex and all of you are formally invited there everyday." He stretched the last word profusely.

"Of course man, I'll be there every night." Vik replied quickly.

"I'm telling everybody, not just you, you would be there anyway, what work you have got?"

"Hey come on Raghav, why the hell are you after my ass all the time?" Vik complained.

"Because you possess one of the laziest asses ever made. Anyway I'll get in your ass later." Raghav turned to face others, "Guys, its something that's finally coming true after years of hard work and endurance, I'm glad I have come so close." His eyes were glinting with satisfaction.

"Great Raghav we are all happy for you, you totally deserve it and we would love to be a part of it." Ruheen said with her graceful smile.

"Another month," Raghav said, "still one more damn month to go." His expression and rhetoric appeared to be the biggest enemies of time. "You know," he continued, "all these years I have been working so damn hard, sleeping only three to four hours a day, doing day jobs, night jobs so that I can get to my best life as early as possible. It all started with that imbecile boss of mine who pestered me all day and I'm so glad I decided to set up something of my own. Today, I can envision it being a reality in some time now." His eyes had the same fire and determination as was a few years back when he first decided on his goal, the same that everybody around him had always seen. They always appeared focussed. Life, he knew, wasn't a piece of cake after all. Neither was success nor the achievement of an ambition. Raghav had learnt that a long time back. He never gave up despite all hardships, just cruised along with a burning desire that kept him heated and charged up for the game called life.

It was during those days, Raghav started inspiring everyone around him. The never daunting spirit, focus, determination was something everyone appreciated in him.

"Raghav just a thought," Rachna asked, "God forbid but what if this idea does not work."

Raghav smiled, "That's alright, success never comes easy, you know what's the most important ingredient to make a recipe called success."

"What?"

Raghav replied, "If I lose, then perhaps it will be better for me."

"How is that?" Rachna asked puzzled.

"Because I'll be more charged up for the next time and who knows maybe I'll get a better idea."

"Hmmmm...."

"You must look at the bright side of everything, only than can you enjoy life." Raghav quipped.

"So have you thought about any other idea?" Purnima inquired.

"You bet, life is full of ideas."

"Alright okay okay." Vik interjected, "That's too much of a philosophy together in a day, not good for my health, Raghav you should consider being a philosopher dude."

"Get lost." Raghav dismissed him.

A minute later, the food arrived – Pasta, lasagne, pizza, iced tea. They were all over it. Ruheen and Nirvaan's eyes met often, but Nirvaan only smiled back. He remembered his words of wisdom that he preached to Raghav and Vik only some time back. He got scared by his own words. The fear came back. He looked at Ruheen momentarily, then poured some ice in his iced tea to cool himself.

"Why are you putting so much ice, the ice tea is already cold, you'll get a bad throat." Ruheen warned.

Oh my God, I was so right. He started taking out the ice immediately with his hand.

"What are you doing, take a damn spoon Nirvaan?" she ordered, "God, you are hopeless."

"Hey hey hey." Vik simpered, "Dude your predictions are coming true, just look at your face."

"What prediction?" Ruheen asked in a huff.

"Oh nothing at all, he's just a big mouth." Nirvaan interjected giving Vik a think - before – you - speak - look.

"No no tell me Vik." Ruheen inquired earnestly.

And so Vik began "When you girls had not come, Nirvaan was telling us how afraid he is of a commitment and especially of you because you would pester him all day and make him life miserable and he was also saying that…….."

Vik stopped midway when he got a knock out glare from Nirvaan, "and nothing else that's what he was saying."

Apart from the terrible laid back attitude of Vik, this was another of his shortcoming. He couldn't keep anything within him especially secrets. In this regard, he was more like his female counterpart, who could never stop gossiping. But they were only slightly better for one, they would never do it in front of the person concerned, back-biting as they call it; and two, they firmly believed that there were still few things which are better untold. But Vik was worse, he could keep nothing at all. On one such occasion, he gushed out the entire list of one of his old friend's girlfriends in front of his present girlfriend. The girl, absolutely stunned, called off the relationship there and then.

After that day, he had formally pledged to all his friends not to share things with him that were meant to be kept as a secret. "Guys please," he had said half heartedly "please don't tell me a secret if you want it to be kept as a secret, I better be unaware than cause another unfortunate break up."

The request from Vik that day, had got everyone burst in a convulsion of laughter.

Today, however, it wasn't a secret, but it was good enough to instill anger in Ruheen and fear in Nirvaan. Nirvaan knew he would have it when they returned home. For now, he avoided looking at her.

There in the backdrop, someone was strumming the guitar. The music was euphoric and soothing to say the least. It filled the air with unmitigated serenity. The six of them turned to look at the guitarist. The guy appeared ordinary with casual clothes but was sure gifted. All the others in the room looked at him too and were spellbound by his playing.

As opposed to Bombay, Goa or East India, guitar was a rarity in Delhi. Only a few Delhites could play it to perfection. Occasionally you could see someone playing a guitar in the open or perhaps at Barista, but that was it. Hence it always drew a lot of attention when someone was in the act in this part of the country. Even a beginner was considered a talented guitarist. No wonder, the guy impressed one and all.

Raghav was particularly impressed. He observed the guitarist avidly. It was so endearing how deftly his fingers moved across the fretboard and it changed the sound. How the pitch of his voice matched with the sound of the guitar. He was playing 'Time of your life' by Green Day. Raghav found it all too fascinating. *Wow I wish I could play like that.* Immediately he took out his diary and under the 6 monthly section wrote 'learn guitar'. He looked at the guitarist again. He struck it off from the 6 monthly section and wrote it under the 3 monthly section.

"What is that Raghav? What did you just write and what is that? A diary isn't it?" Purnima asked as she observed him writing.

"Yeah, right my diary." he replied.

"Can I have a look at that?"

"Sure."

He handed it over to Purnima.

'THINGS TO DO BEFORE I DIE', the cover of the diary said unabashedly in big block letters. Purnima read the title aloud. Everyone rose on their seats. This was something very new to them. They grew excited as Purnima went on with its description.

The diary was divided into four sections – monthly, 3 monthly, yearly and 3 yearly. Under every section were a list of items written, their date of entry and in some of them the date of completion which Raghav successfully achieved. They were struck off by a single straight line. Invariably Purnima noticed that the date of completion for a task never exceeded its time limit. One such case was an item under the three monthly section that read – 'learn to cook Italian food' on 22.09.09 and the date of completion was 10.12.09.

"Whatever you decide to do in a particular span of time, you always complete it within that time, is it?" Purnima asked in a tone that was brimming with appreciation and admiration.

"Not always." Raghav replied with pride and a wink "Sometimes I complete it in less time than allotted but never more."

"So you cook Italian food, huh."

"Yes I have ventured a bit in that field." said Raghav.

"But why only Italian?" Rachna asked.

"Ah well." Raghav replied making a squelching sound. "I have always been an ardent fan of anything Italian. A few years back Vik and I were having dinner at a restaurant called Flavors in Defence Colony. The food was exquisite to say the least and the variety colossal. It struck me then that I must learn how to master Italian cuisine."

"Guys you should eat the lasagne that Raghav cooks, it'll leave an indelible impression on your taste buds, truly out of this world" Vik said.

"Alright Raghav, you sure owe us a meal then." Purnima said overexcited as she continued reading further.

"But Raghav tell me something." Rachna inquired, "Why do you have to write everything in your dairy."

Raghav smiled, "You know what Rachna, the wisest of people write the smallest of things."

"Really?"

"Besides," he continued, "I feel it is the best way to keep a track of all that I want to do. It gives me the direction to head and frankly it has made my life more organized and fulfilling."

"Hmm .... alright." Purnima hummed as she continued reading aloud the activities that Raghav vowed to pursue. They included a vacation to Bahamas, learn horse riding, learn flying, a trip to space, run a school for the blind, write a book, etc.

"Oh you want to write a book as well1" Purnima shrieked, thrilled by the idea.

"Yeah," Raghav replied "I'll start working on it from the next month onwards, once things are settled with my club. I'm really looking forward to this one."

"But what would you write on?" Vik asked in bewilderment, "The toughest part about writing a book is to decide what to write on."

"Yeah I know," Raghav replied, "but I have already figured that out."

"Oh is it?" Purnima fluttered "Then tell us what it will be about."

The fact that Purnima was truly and completely engrossed in Raghav's diary was evident in the mirror being totally ignored. For a while atleast, she wasn't bothered about it.

"Well," Raghav marvelled, "It will be a story about us, our dreams, our passion and how we go about achieving it."

"Wow a book1" Vik wondered, "Damn why didn't I get that idea."

"Well Vik I always tell you, you need the right vision to see through the countless ideas that life has bestowed upon us. Trust me the ideas are multitudinous only if you thinks so."

"And you want to learn flying too!" Purnima interjected, heedless to what Raghav said.

"Yup, I have always been fascinated about planes soaring high in the sky. It would be breathtaking really to command and fly a thing like that. I believe it is one of the most innovative and awe inspiring invention of man."

"Yeah I totally agree on that." Purnima replied.

"You know what Raghav" Rachna said after being quiet for a while and being a good listener as good as she claimed Mishi to be. "I don't think there will be anybody in this world who would want to do so many things in his life, and you just added guitar today."

Raghav smiled nonchalantly, "You know what Rachna fifty years down the line when I'll be lying on my deathbed, I won't be regretting that I haven't done or seen or experienced something. I would have done all that I desired. And then there on my deathbed, I'll close my eyes in peace and revel in the fact that there's nothing left in this world to live for."

"Hmm . . ." Purnima thought soulfully, "and we would be doing just the opposite of it, blaming and criticizing ourselves that we should have been a bit serious about life."

"But still Raghav," Rachna continued, "I feel you are living your life as though this is your last year."

"Yeah true." Raghav replied, "Some wise men have said that if you want to extract everything out of life, then live as if today is your last day, I'm still being slow in assuming that this year is my last ."

Rachna didn't say anything after that. She appeared convinced.

"And you know what guys," Raghav continued, "there was a time in my life when everything was hunky dory, there was no better place than this world, I had a song on my lips wherever I went, clear blue sky, lush green grass, cool breeze that caressed me, but then something really horrible and obnoxious happened and my life was torn apart."

"Oh what was that? What happened?" Ruheen asked concerned.

"I fell in love."

"What?" She shrieked as she jumped off her chair. She never expected that answer.

"Yeah I fell in love with a girl who was cold blooded and cold hearted to the extent that it never really mattered to her whether I existed or not."

"And then what happened?"

"I wasted four and a half years until I realized she was a tough nut to crack. After finally getting over her I realized what a foolish person I had been to fall in love and let my life revolve around her."

Everyone listened to Raghav carefully and patiently. Even Nirvaan who had a hatred for love stories seemed captivated.

"All these things that I have written in my diary" Raghav continued, "were my interests or hobbies as you may say since my school days, but after I fell in love with her, everything felt minuscule. Years later after my final break up, I swore to myself that from now on nothing would hold me back from chasing my passions and goals."

Everyone was silent. A faint smile hovered on their faces.

"And that's why" Raghav added, "I want to make up for the time I lost and proceed in my life in fifth gear. I am just waiting for my club to get set, and then I'll be on top of all that I have written in my diary."

"Wow Raghav," Ruheen said with a vivid smile "whatever people think I must say I like your attitude. How many of us chase our goals like this?" she cocked her head as she spoke to everybody. "I mean everyone of us thinks about it, but we either don't have the will power or time management. Raghav I must say I am impressed."

"Thanks," Raghav replied, "but you know what, it actually depends on how passionate you are about something. After that tragic love story of mine, my passion has always been to pursue all my passions, the first one is of course to set up my own business. And then a string of other little dreams flooded my brain and I had to resort to writing so that I don't forget even one of them."

"Yeah Raghav we know, Things to do before I die stands proof." Vik replied.

"Right." Raghav said "Guys I feel life is meant to be happy and content and you can be both only if all your dreams are fulfilled and for that you must work. Like look at this idiot Vik." he gave Vik a glance of scorn. "He's been telling me since years that one day he would do something big but till date he hasn't even thought about it."

He looked at Vik again. "You think you will ever be happy until you achieve something like that."

Vik was quiet. "Yeah alright I'll see."

"Dude, life is short, really short, you have to be on your toes if you want to achieve something."

"Well its not that short." Vik replied.

"Oh never mind just let it be, you are impossible."

Raghav could sense that everybody except Vik was engaged in thought. They seemed impressed. His words left a mark on them somewhere.

"I'll also keep a diary from now on and write everything that I want to do in it" Purnima said excitedly.

Everyone smiled and looked at her. They could see her list clearly – improve my hair style, hair quality, work on my looks, my gait, my figure.

"Just make sure you add an item of 'think at times'." Raghav laughed.

14

THE FASHION WEEK....

Rachna's day had arrived. The fashion week for which she had waited anxiously for months had finally come. The Hotel Grand in Vasant Kunj had the honour of hosting the event. It had been a successful four days of the fashion week and today was the last day. Rachna's collection would be showcased just before the Grand Finale and she knew right from the onset, that indeed, this was her day.

Swanky cars kept coming in every minute in the huge and opulent porch of the Hotel as they were led in valet parking. They carried bejewelled fashion designers, celebrities, fashion icons and the whos who of the fashion industry. And the media of course to capture, cover it all.

The whole ambience had a trance like tranquillity that was further accentuated by the sensuous smell of the flowers that flooded the embankment on either side of the atrium.

Minutes before commencement of the show, Raghav and friends reached the Grand. Raghav brought the car to a screeching halt as he studied his options of parking the vehicle. He proceeded to the basement parking at the behest of Ruheen.

"Guys fast." he yelled "Rachna's show would be on anytime."

Purnima and Ruheen had a final glance at themselves in the tinted window shields of the car before being beckoned forcefully by the three guys to the elevator. To their fantasy and the guy's misfortune, the elevator had mirrors on all sides.

It had taken almost a month and few trips to the shopping malls for Ruheen and Purnima to decide what to wear for the occasion. Ruheen had chosen a red dress with a plunging neckline and matched it immaculately with red pumps. She put up her hair in a high knot ponytail. She looked like a perfect angel much like the fashion goddesses that flanked the Grand. She hoped Nirvaan would think as much.

Purnima wore a short skirt and a halter top with black stilettos almost six inches to manage her to reach at least up to the waist of the models. She highlighted her eye lashes with mascara and painted her nails with bright red nail polish. She did her hair with crystal embedded hair clips. She too, looked like a little angel.

The boys, all three of them, wore a blue jeans and a black shirt. Period.

Ruheen's efforts to look stunning had an ephemeral effect on Nirvaan and it lasted until the elevator doors opened. They observed the floor was swamped by the biggies of the fashion industry. It was a wonderful sight, especially for Nirvaan who almost swooned when he saw a horde of beautiful women around him.

"Why the hell am I not a fashion designer?" he said to himself.

It was already six and SnS's show was to begin right then. They headed towards the hall depriving Nirvaan of his lascivious glares at the most gorgeous women he had seen in his life, much to the relief of Ruheen. They handed their passes to the guard as they entered the massive hall. The hall was huge and had a makeshift T-shaped ramp at its centre. Chairs were arranged orderly around it with no access to the first three rows as that was the prerogative of the bigwigs of the industry. Raghav pointed towards five chairs that lied vacant. It offered a panoramic view of the ramp in front. They made themselves comfortable on them.

"Wow this setting looks brilliant, isn't it guys?" Purnima said.

"Of course" Nirvaan beamed. His eyes looked sideways, ahead, backwards and everywhere wherever his owl like eyes could manoeuvre. To his dismay or excitement, he found beauty everywhere he looked. It was heaven.

"Where is Rachna?" Vik asked.

"Oh she must be backstage helping the models to get ready." Purnima replied.

Oh! The models. Nirvaan yearned, licking his lips.

The fashion show commenced with a speech from an elderly gentlemen representing SnS. He was tall and lean, bald with neatly trimmed beard. His rhetoric was very impressive as he regaled the audience with his subtle, often dark humour. His extempore speech went on for roughly fifteen minutes but the audience never got the feeling of boredom. On the contrary, they enjoyed it and his speech culminated with a huge round of applause.

Thereafter the ramp was on fire with the most gorgeous and beautiful models of the country walking on it. They walked with such poise and confidence that it got the audience right on the edge of their seats. There was a soothing background music that caressed the air. Nirvaan stared at the models lecherously with a gaping mouth and eyes that were popping out. Ruheen who sat next to him observed him in his act. When she looked at him, his tongue went in and the eyes contracted slightly. They regained their position and size respectively when Ruheen turned away.

"Wow these models look so pretty," Purnima said "I wish I could be one of them."

"Sure Purnima why not?" Vik replied, "But you have to be only a foot taller to be able to do that."

"Oh no Pooh" Raghav contributed "you could still be there, child models do equally well."

Purnima showed the middle finger of both her hands, one for Raghav and the other for Vik. She followed it up with an inconceivable guffaw.

"Guys you are so funny" she remarked.

Backstage Rachna received an order to meet Kazi immediately. She felt a trickle of nervousness. *Damn him.* For her it was a sign of evil omen to see *the fighter* before her show. *Damn his dirty, shitty face.*

"So Rachna," Kazi spoke in a high pitched voice that was fierce and uncouth. "Is everything set, it's your turn in the next ten minutes."

"Sir I am all ready and up for it." Rachna replied looking away from his grouchy face.

"You better be." Kazi fired. "I don't want any mishaps, you still have some time, ensure all is well or you are in for a tough time."

Bastard. "Right Sir."

Kazi stood there staring right into her eyes with admonishment. It didn't comfort Rachna. She avoided any eye contact and took a deep breath. She considered the option of reprising her act she had done in his office few days back, but then decided against it as she had more important things to take care of. *Some other time, watch out for your nose asshole.*

"Alright you can go now, get everything organized, I want it perfect, no setbacks alright." Kazi warned, "no setbacks."

"Sir." Rachna replied and vanished a second later.

The show continued with the ramp walk of lanky models adorned with new and innovative designs. The last ramp walk for SnS was of Rachna's Fall Winter contemporary collection. Ruheen and Purnima waited anxiously for it. They tried to catch a glimpse of Rachna by looking around to wish her luck, but they know she would be backstage doing the final bit of her preparation. Both of them knew how important a day it was for her. She had to impress her fellow designers. Somehow, both of them knew Rachna would be successful as she had been totally up to it right from the onset. And then of course, they knew, there would be no stopping her. They wished her luck.

The models representing Rachna's designs were finally out on the ramp. They were beautiful models with loads of attitude and a check - me - out demeanour. Their costumes looked majestic to say the least and they flashed with the hard work Rachna had put in. When the show was done, the crowd erupted and acknowledged it with a big applause. Rachna emerged from backstage and was overwhelmed with the appreciation. She thanked her models and bowed to the crowd. She ran her eyes quickly through the people seated in front. Each one of them had their hands together and a good-work-done look on their face. Rachna knew at once she had done it.

To her consternation, Rachna saw a smile even on Kazi's face and he was clapping. *Oh god is it true.* And she knew it was. Kazi was smiling and applauding and his moustache slithered with pride.

The show ended with a Grand Finale which consisted of a ramp walk of the models along with their respective designers. Confetti was sprayed all over the floor and soon it was decorated with bright colours. The show finally ended with a huge applause.

Rachna was at her stall when her friends emerged from behind. She was being congratulated by her colleagues and senior designers. The smile never left her face.

"Hey guys," she leapt forward as she raw Ruheen and Purnima. "How did you find my show?"

"It was perfect, couldn't have been better." Ruheen replied as Purnima nodded.

"And boys what do you say?"

"Oh phenomenal, excellent." Nirvaan exclaimed looking at a model ahead of him.

"Nirvaan I was talking about the show."

"So that's what I said."

"Oh never mind, guys I am just hoping that a buyer approaches me, that will be the perfect end to this evening."

"I'm sure of that." Purnima said.

"Alright guys, go have some drinks, enjoy yourself, I have some work to do, will see you all later."

They proceeded to the drinks corner. Nirvaan continued looking around him ogling all the girls. If Ruheen hadn't been around, he would have surely spelt his charm on some of them or at least tried. Ruheen who stood beside him wasn't totally unaware of what welled inside Nirvaan's flirtatious mind.

'Does he even love me?' was all she thought. Her eyes traced a path that followed Nirvaan's line of sight. And every time she noticed , it stopped on a 'hot chick's' body as Nirvann's words for a pretty girl. His eyes did a few rounds up and down her body stopping at her strategic locations and then they moved over to another similar site.

Raghav was aware of what went around him. He observed the expression of depression on Ruheen's face. In between, the depressed look gave way to a sullen one which made her face a bright red fuming with anger, but owing to the people around, the depressed look always returned. Raghav hoped that Ruheen didn't put expressed her feelings there as it would create a scene that was surely unwanted. He looked at Nirvaan and tried his best to make him understand that 'dude you'll be in deep shit soon'. But Nirvaan never bothered to look at him.

"Excuse me." Ruheen said awash with anger and sadness "I'll just be back."

"Where are you going Ruheen ?" Purnima asked "Wait I'll come along."

Raghav waited for the girls to disappear. "What the hell are you up to?" he yelled when they were gone.

"What?" Nirvaan replied puzzled.

Vik smiled and patted his back "Dude you had it today."

They left Grand an hour later. Rachna was busy with her clients and colleagues so she asked them to carry on. It had been a long day for her. Nirvaan was not in the slightest mood to leave. He was beckoned by Raghav and Vik towards the car. Ruheen's anger and unease was perceivable in her silence as she smouldered within. She didn't utter a word in their one hour drive from Grand to their place. Raghav was aware of it. So was Nirvaan.

"Guys do you know who I met when you people left? Rachna screamed as soon as she entered the house. Her eyes had become double their size, pupils had dilated and there was an unmistakable glow on her face that characterized her excitement.

Purnima and Ruheen raised their brows in anticipation. Just when they were about to ask Rachna, she screamed again. "The Invogue Company of Germany," she came towards Mishi who jumped and whisked in the water in empathy with Rachna's feelings. Rachna poured her some food. "So where was I?" she asked as she cavorted about the floor "Yeah their manager who was at the show came up to me and offered a freelance project."

Purnima and Ruheen listened sympathetically and seemed overjoyed. "He said their company needs a young and innovative designer like me for the designs for their spring summer' 2012 collection in three months time."

"Great news Rachna, well done." Ruheen said.

"Yeah and he has given me about six weeks to prepare those designs. Nothing has been finalised yet though, I have to see him again tomorrow and he is leaving India the day after."

They congratulated her and so did Mishi in her own way.

"And the best part is" Rachna continued still screaming "I don't even have to leave my job for this and of course." she paused to draw a deep breath "the money is great too."

"Fantastic really!"

"I know."

"So we expect a busier Rachna from tomorrow?" Ruheen asked.

"Tomorrow, no way." Rachna corrected. "Today, infact now, right now I'll be into it. I can't afford to waste any time now that I see my fashion designer dream dead ahead of me."

And with that she scurried inside her room.

Mishi continued jumping and cavorting in the water so hard that some water spilled out of the bowl.

Her happiness knew no bounds.

15
THE ADVICE !!!

Ruheen waited anxiously on the first floor of Barista at PVR Priya, Vasant Vihar. It had been roughly twenty five minutes since she had been sitting there desperately waiting for him to arrive. The Saturday evening was crisp and pleasant and the air was filled with the sensuous fragrance of the flowers that surrounded the complex. This place had become a dating joint really over the last few years as invariably the entire complex swarmed with couples of all age groups. Boys and girls and occasionally boys and boys walked hand in hand as they strolled past the multitudinous stores and shops that stretched along the entire length of the complex on either side. There was always a healthy hustle around the complex and a big long queue that stretched ahead of the ticket counter of PVR and another queue waiting for the entry into the huge hall.

Inside Barista, Ruheen checked her watch. It said 6:35pm. "Damn." she said it had been more than half an hour now. She looked around the place. People of all age groups were engrossed in their coffee and conversation with their better or perhaps bitter halves. She allowed herself a smile. *Wonder if Nirvaan would be as happy as these couples when he's with me.* She could never really figure out his feelings. She wondered if she had ever met a person in her life more unpredictable than him. She remembered it was he who had initiated their relationship. It was he who had moved his lips close to hers on their first kiss. It was his idea of having an affair. *Then what happened to him after that.* Perhaps it all went too fast and Nirvaan couldn't match the pace of Ruheen as she worked as a catalyst from there on to which their relationship catapulted. Not that Ruheen was unaware of Nirvaan's feelings, but the unconditional love she had for him was irrevocable. Even a thought of his tore open her face in a wide and full smile. The anger she had for him on the day of the fashion week had receded in a few hours.

"Tuck Tuck" she heard the sound of timber next to her that made her wake up from her reverie.

"Hey Raghav you finally came, huh." she blurted in a low voice.

"Yup, sorry about the time." Raghav smiled as he sat down.

"Oh never mind."

They ordered coffee and sandwiches.

"What happened Ruheen, is everything okay? Why did you want to meet me alone?"

"Sure don't worry, all is well."

Ruheen knew Raghav was the perfect guy for this. He could understand the feelings of a girl as closely as that of a guy. Even in the past it was he along with Purnima who had stood by her in her endeavour of waiting for Nirvaan. It was he who gave her all the support and advice to stay calm and composed. He was the only guy in whom she confided.

Though everything had been just about alright in Ruheen and Nirvaan's relationship except for the commitment factor and a few rifts here and there, Ruheen knew she wasn't in for a bright future. Nirvaan's craving for females, the lust in his eyes was something that made her apprehensive of her future. 'Does he even love me?' was the penultimate question that always ran through her mind and deprived her of sleep for nights together. She wanted to be sure she was justified in still waiting for him and wanted to read Nirvaan's mind from a guy's perspective. And boy, she thought, do I have a better choice than Raghav.

"Ruheen go on." Raghav said as though reading her mind "What do you want to know about Nirvaan?"

"Thanks," she muttered "thanks Raghav for understanding."

"Anytime, now go on."

Whenever she spoke about Nirvaan, her cheeks went scarlet, eyes deep and fresh, full of vigour. Nothing in her life would give her more pleasure than merely talking about Nirvaan. But today Raghav noted her precisely as she spoke. There was a careworn edge to her voice. She flinched nervously at times and the words trembled out from her mouth. It was as if there was somebody inside her restricting her speech. Her eyes were dark and gloomy, they had lost their brightness and appeared dull and tired.

"I don't know if that asshole even loves me" she was saying in a depressed voice "you saw him on the fashion week day, didn't you? The ass couldn't keep his eyes off a single girl and that was when I was right next to him, wonder what he would have done if I wasn't there."

"Alright Ruheen take it easy." Raghav interrupted. He knew exactly where she was heading. Had he allowed her to continue, tears would surely have found their way out of her moist eyes. And the unease they bring to every guy, he knew, was something no girl could ever understand.

"Look Ruheen, I totally understand what you say, but you can't force Nirvaan into anything. If it he's not ready for a commitment you have to accept the fact." Raghav looked closely into Ruheen's eyes. There was still time. He was in a philosophical mood today "Love is unconditional, you can't have expectations from it, because if you do then it's not love, but a compromise."

"But I don't have any expectations from him." Ruheen complained.

"Yes you do, the very fact that you ask for a commitment from him is an expectation, the feeling for a commitment should come from within and not be enforced."

Ruheen was silent. She knew Raghav had a point. But what was she to do. She needed him at any cost and with a commitment.

"Look Ruheen," Raghav continued as gracefully and politely as he could "I should not say Nirvaan is not worthy of your love, but get it straight across that it's good to love someone, but you shouldn't allow that person to define your life. Your happiness and sadness should be in your hands and not at the mercy of or at the whims and fancies of the person you love. Because when that happens you cease to enjoy life."

Raghav took a break for a while. He gave some time to Ruheen to absorb what he said. She creased her brows and her worries seamed to grow. She gave him a despondent look.

"Alright Ruheen, you remember I told you guys once about my tragic love story. I think I need to put light on that again."

Ruheen signalled him to continue.

"When I was in school I was madly and deeply in love with a classmate of mine. So much that nothing, absolutely nothing else in this world mattered to me. For five long years I waited for her and everything else—my studies, career, passions had taken a back seat. And then one fine day she left me just like that."

Ruheen observed the smile that was a characteristic of Raghav's face had diminished. His voice grew hollow and solemn.

"She defined my life completely. Everything I did, I thought, I wanted revolved around her. I cried, I laughed, I smiled at her disposal. And the day she left me I was marooned and abandoned, the pain it bought along, pierced my heart and soul for days and months and years." Raghav closed his eyes and pressed his fingers to his temple.

"So you see Ruheen," he continued in a low, husky voice "I won't call that a sensible idea. Now when I look back I feel that I lost those five damned years. I could have used them more wisely and sensibly, in a way I can say I have learnt a lesson. Never be so attached to someone that you get detached from the world and more importantly from yourself."

Ruheen nodded. "I understand Raghav, but tell me what do I do?"

"Alright," Raghav said getting rid of his past by shaking his head violently, "first things first, promise me that whatever said and done your life will not revolve around him, you will be responsible for your happiness and sadness and not him."

"I'll try."

"Please do and secondly you won't have any expectations from him."

"I'll try that as well."

"Good"

"But tell me something Raghav, how do you find Nirvaan? Do you think its sensible for me to wait for him? I don't know but this feels like an eternity."

Difficult question. Raghav was puzzled. He did not think highly about Nirvaan. Deep down, he himself felt it wasn't a wonderful idea to wait for a nut like him. Girls defined his life and Raghav could never imagine him getting settled with a single woman for life and be happy thereafter. He remembered the day when he had gone out for a survey for his club to find out if girls would be interested in it along with Nirvaan and Vik. That bastard, he thought, made the best of the opportunity and got hold of a girl for himself and after that discussion he had with him at Big Chill about Ruheen, it could sure be an eternal wait.

"Tell me Raghav what do you think?" Ruheen asked impatiently.

"What do you want me to say Ruheen?" he asked. He was still not sure how to frame his words. Different ideas conjured in his mind as he put them off, waiting for the perfect one.

He finally spoke slowly and carefully, "Alright, I feel you have already given him enough time, haven't you?"

Ruheen nodded.

"So it would be best that you give him a final period to decide, say three months, beyond which I definitely suggest you should move on."

"Move on, are you serious?" Ruheen's jaw dropped.

"Yeah, but first give him the last bit of time."

But how am I supposed to move on. All those months, those feelings and emotions, forget them, just like that. A little tear escaped Ruheen's eyes.

"You are good Ruheen, you deserve a better guy than him."

"Sometimes you know Raghav, I think as much, but it's not as easy as it seems."

"It's not easy because you think so. It's all in your mind. But the day you decide against it, you'll be a different person, trust me."

Ruheen had nothing to say. The last year had been a cracker of a year love, hatred, anger, patience, defiance; it had tested all her emotions. It was a medley of feelings that saw her moaning and writhing in pain as much as overflowing with happiness. But the wait had been killing.

A wave of confusion swept over her as she held her head with both hands, scratching it to give rest to her mind.

"Relax Ruheen, take it easy." Raghav advised "There is something vital about guys that I feel you must know."

Ruheen was all ears.

"Always remember the importance and affection you give your guy is inversely proportional to the importance and affection you get."

"*What? Say* that again."

"Yeah, I always see you concerned about Nirvaan's comfort and happiness, you do things to convince him, but I think you shouldn't be. Don't let him take you for granted, send shivers and tremors down his spine when he's with you, be unpredictable, be capricious, be fidgety, be finicky, make unreasonable demands and then make sure you get them fulfilled. Argue with him, fight with him, trouble him, torture him, be like his boss, be deadly, be a ghost, to sum it all – be the *fernme fatale.*"

Ruheen was all ears.

"Guys love the femininity in their girls. Mollycoddling and being mushy all the time is a turn off. Always keep him guessing what you would be up to next, don't share everything with him. Keep a certain amount of distance from him, play with his emotions, tantalize him, slap him, kick him, to sum it all – be a girl."

Ruheen was all ears.

"Alright I agree you do some of the stuff I mentioned, but you should practise it regularly. Though I know there is a part of Nirvaan that is afraid of you but I want his entire self to be afraid, I hope you are getting what I mean?"

Ruheen wore a confused look. "What are you saying? Do you want me to break up with him?"

"Oh no, no," Raghav protested, "just do it, he'll come back to you."

"And what if he doesn't?"

"Then you have to give up on him, take your call, move on."

"Right." Ruheen girded herself.

"Good."

She looked at Raghav lovingly. "I hope you know, you are the best."

"Yeah people say so."

"Seriously Raghav you have been great, always a true friend, thanks for being with me."

"Anytime."

"And I wish you all the very best in all your endeavours, I am sure D'CoBo club will rock."

"You bet."

Ruheen nodded. "Alright then, I'll give him his last three months to decide."

"Excellent."

'Three months then'. Ruheen wondered.

Little did she know that three months was too much a time she had planned to give Nirvaan.

16

BAD, VERY BAD, VERY VERY BAD BOYFRIENDS!!!

"Can I ask you something?" Ruheen said, perplexed, looking straight into his eyes.

"Sure go ahead" he replied. *As though I have a choice.*

"Do you love me?"

Terrible question. Nirvaan wasn't sure why she always kept popping the same question time and again. Of course, he thought he did, but what was he to tell her 'yeah babe I do but who's going to take care of the other girls' or maybe 'yeah sure I love you but what if tomorrow I find a better girl.'

Nirvaan felt horrible, a familiar unease gripped him. Not many options, he thought.

"Of course I do" he replied keeping the other ideas to himself.

"Then why the hell are you taking so much time to decide?" Ruheen fired her second question imperiously which took Nirvaan by surprise.

Another bad question. Nirvaan pondered.

Man why can't people understand there is all the time in the world to decide, what's the damn hurry?

Dare I say that?

"Because you know honey I want to be sure if I'm sure."

"God! don't get started with that sure thing again, you know I hate you for that, damn! you are the worst boyfriend ever, a very very bad boyfriend."

Oh really. Nirvaan had heard that a million times and each time far more pronounced than the previous one.

According to Ruheen, Purnima and Rachna, boyfriends are always classified in three categories: bad, very bad and very very bad. The one who is given the tag of a bad boyfriend is actually the best of the lot. It never gets any better than that.

Nirvaan had experienced a feeling of pride and achievement a few months back when he was termed a 'bad boyfriend.' "Wow, I am the best!" he had hoarded the tag self righteously for a few days till Ruheen changed her mind.

Today he was the worst. But deep down he himself knew he wasn't a good one either. He understood that she loved him most dearly. Her parents were after her to get married. To pester him, he knew, wasn't absolutely unreasonable. But what else was he supposed to do. If he told her the truth, she would be hurt big time. Moreover he himself never wanted to lose her. Sure he lusted for every pretty girl that came his way but he still had something special for her somewhere deep in his heart.

'Some more time maybe', he thought. He looked at Ruheen. She too was lost in her thoughts.

I think Raghav is right, it is high time I must decide what to do. This seems to be an endless wait. He will never be sure of himself. But more than deciding, Ruheen knew she was only consoling herself. To forget him would be the hardest task for her and to do that without getting an answer, even harder.

Suddenly Raghav's words came back to her. She immediately woke up. "Three months" she blurted.

"What?" Nirvaan stared at her in horror.

"Yes three months." Ruheen asserted "I'm giving you the last three months to decide." she paused "if you decide by then I'll be there for you but if you don't, then piss off and screw yourself." She punched the table producing a thudding sound.

"What happened to you?" Nirvaan stared in bewilderment.

"Yup I can't take it any longer." She stood up quickly to leave "Three months." she yelled and left in a huff.

Nirvaan sat there all by himself, wondering 'if she had really said that.'

17

THE CRAVING FOR *DAARU*!!!

Rachna lay in her bedroom stretching her hands and feet languorously. It had been more than an hour since she had returned from office still it felt like barely five minutes. She longed for a good body massage as she was awfully tired. The fashion week had ended three weeks back. As she had sworn to herself that it would be the defining moment of her life, it pretty well turned out to be. She got two freelance offers from Indian companies and one from an international buyer—Invogue. Her work began very well as she toiled day and night. But today she was tired not because of work. Last night it had been an overdose of booze and partying.

The day after the fashion week, the international buyer of Invogue, Germany met in person with Rachna. He was a tall man with dark, brooding eyes. He spoke gently with a euphonious voice often juxtaposed with humour. His eyes lit up every time following his own dark sarcasm.

"So Rachna, how's it going?" Niel asked

"Fantastic to say the least." *Getting to meet an international buyer after my first show, fan-fuckin-tastic!*

He told Rachna that he was far more than impressed with her innovative and chic designs and the purpose of his visit to India was served. The Spring Summer' 12 collection of his company, he said, was in the pipeline.

"I was wondering" Niel asked casually, "if you would be interested in making the designs for the same."

Rachna was taken aback. She was swept off her feet. *Are you serious man?*

"Of course, I'll make sure you get a good sum for the same."
You must be kidding.

Rachna was overwhelmed with the offer. Getting such an offer almost immediately wasn't entirely impossible, but sure wasn't an unheard of feat. Nevertheless she grabbed it with both hands.

"I'll be more than glad to work with your company." she announced unequivocally.

Though Rachna hadn't really heard of the company, the German tag alone was enough to send adrenaline pumping through her body. It was not just the money but also the exposure to the international market. The experience she would get was something she had been looking forward to. It would go a long way getting close to her fashion designer dream. And the best part – she wasn't required to leave her job in SnS. True it involved a lot of hard work and burning the midnight lamp, but she knew she was totally up for it. *I think I should stop sleeping from now on, would sleep next once I am an established designer.*

"So," Niel asked, raising his bushy eyebrows "do I consider it deal then?"

"Of course."

"Alright then, here's my card, call me for any queries. I will be leaving India soon, so I'll see you tomorrow and discuss all about the designs."

"Sure."

Rachna was ecstatic when she reached home that day. She was brimming with happiness Mishi had ever seen before. Rachna's excitement got her panting and pounding through the water. Purnima and Ruheen too, were thrilled.

The next day after her office hours, Rachna went straight to visit Niel. Excitement had taken away all the tiredness that had crept in her body after the day's work. She reached their designated rendezvous place right on time. Niel greeted her warmly.

Niel took off with a brief introduction about his company followed by his own little introduction. His accent was heavy punctuated with sarcasm which Rachna initially found hard to fathom. But the expression offered by his face aided Rachna. She observed he had a very positive attitude towards life and had high expectations from himself and also others around him. In a way, she thought he resembled Raghav who himself unleashed positive vibes wherever he went. Rachna tried to concentrate.

"So Rachna you must know that the Spring Summer' 12 collection would be held in three months from now."

"Right Niel."

"And we can give you not more than six weeks time to prepare your designs."

Six weeks is more than enough time, I don't need even that much, come on Niel. "Sure. Six weeks will be good."

"Great."

The following hour they discussed everything about the designs Rachna was expected to come up with. Niel asked her to prepare three separate and distinct collections for the season comprising of at least five to six styles in each collection. But before even coming to the designs, she had to do research work in fashion forecasting the season—fabrics to be used, colour combination and trends of the season. Though it appeared to be an arduous task because of the limited time period granted, Rachna had no qualms about her credentials and abilities. Nor did Niel.

After their discussion Rachna was asked to clarify any doubts. "None, it's all understood Niel, you don't worry, I'll call you after six weeks with my designs."

"Marvellous, I'll look forward to them." Niel said in a sanguine tone "And if our company approves them, you will be flooded with a horde of other assignments."

Rachna chuffed. She jumped to her feet at once. "I think I should take your leave then, I'm in no mood to waste even a second." *The life I have always wanted awaits me.*

"Right." Niel wished her luck and bid her goodbye.

When she reached home, her heart was beating faster. It still felt like a dream and she was in no mood to spoil it. She told Ruheen, Purnima and Mishi about the day's events and they were elated. She scurried to her room and opened the fridge to pull out a beer but suddenly decided against it. "Oh no it's just a matter of six weeks. Can't waste my time like this." She scrambled towards her bed and pulled out a diary and a pen from the drawer. She began organizing a time table for herself for the coming six weeks. And she knew it right then this was not going to be a piece of cake. 'Six weeks could be a touch short' she thought. She cancelled the six hours sleep she had allotted herself and substituted it with four. After finalizing her time table, she kept her diary aside and began researching on the net. Since this was her first night, she decided it would be the longest. She evaded sleep for the entire night but finally gave in sleeping the last two hours before getting ready for office. In the morning she was tired and exhausted but never out of focus and discipline. The burning desire she had within kept her going.

In office, she did her job without a shade of indifference. Instead she was all the more enthusiastic and energetic. She anxiously waited for the evening when she would be home preparing the designs.

When she returned home, she didn't allow herself a second of rest and was right over the designs. She barely slept two hours for the second consecutive night. The schedule went on pretty much the similar way for the next two weeks. She did good to match the pace with the time that ticked away. But it was the third week when things started changing. Her performance began nose diving, partly owing to the work pressure and partly due to her craving for alcohol. She couldn't concentrate much in the office and ruminated for long hours. *'Is this so important that I miss all my fun for it.'* Surprisingly it was only a small part within her that was in disagreement.

Her evenings that were allotted for the designs shared their duration with booze and towards the end of the third week were totally expunged from her schedule. *What's life without daaru, god I missed it so much.*

The clubbing era returned as she found herself drinking every second day in a pub. On evenings when she wasn't in a pub, she remembered Niel, her designs and her dream in a blur. "Oh never mind later." she uttered to herself shunning the thoughts. "I have all the time in the world to do that." When she came out of the pub to get back to her place, she collided with Raghav and Vik.

"Guys what are you doing here?" she asked in an alcoholic haze.

"Had to meet Roshan, he's the one renting out the place for my pub."

"Now?" She looked at her watch "isn't it late?" she asked dizzily.

"Yeah I know, but he's a night person."

"Right I see." she said inebriated and what about D'CoBo club, when is that opening?"

"Exactly seven days later, the next Saturday." Raghav replied in a tone of pride and achievement.

"Hey great man, so finally your dream of seven years has come down to seven days, huh".

"Of course it has, I tell you I am so excited and nervous at the same time." he looked at Vik who nodded.

"Just relax, I'm sure it will be good."

"We'll see, anyway what about your work, Ruheen told us you got a freelance project to be done in six weeks."

"Yeah I know, but count out the three weeks from that, they are gone." Rachna yawned.

"So what's happening now, are you already done with it?" Raghav asked.

"You must be insane, I haven't touched it since the last week."

Raghav was taken aback. "And you seem proud of it."

"No it's just that I can't be working like this throughout, have to enjoy my life as well, I'll do it some other time."

Strange this wasn't the Rachna I had known. When did she start speaking like Vik? Or was it the Vik effect. "Rachna I thought you were hell bent to achieve your dream just like me." "Yeah I know" she sighed "but there's no time for me this way, I can't compromise for fun, besides I have all the time in the world to pursue my dream, I can think about that later, what's the hurry?"

Vik winked. *That's my girl.*

"God you are walking on Vik's footsteps Rachna, beware, life is short, really short, you have to be on your toes if you want to achieve something in life."

"Yeah I know you always say that." Rachna yawned again" But right now my feet are hurting, I need to get back home and sleep."

Raghav and Vik bid her good bye. They came a few metres ahead when Vik bellowed behind Raghav, "See it's not just I who think like that."

"I hope God teaches you guys a lesson" Raghav replied shaking his head.

When she reached home, Rachna slumped on her bed and fell asleep seconds later. Her sketches that she had started making for the designs were lying on the far end of the table, crumpled and abandoned. Mishi slouched at the bottom of the bowl. She didn't seem impressed.

18

ALMOST THERE!!!!!!

The evening was the brightest Raghav had ever seen, the breeze the coolest he had ever felt, the babel the most meloderies he had ever heard. For a moment it felt like he was in paradise. The spectacle presented to him was unprecedented. It felt great, it felt wonderful; it was an out of this world experience. D'CoBo club was over crowded and swarmed with people as boys and girls alike kept pouring in every minute. Raghav and Vik had a tough time managing them.

"Oh God so many people, so many people, wow!" Raghav was yelling amidst the clatter of a thousand other voices. "Vik can you believe it man, I did it, God I did it."

"Yeah," Vik shouted, "this is heavenly dude, we have succeeded."

'But how do I control these people, there's going to be a stampede this way.' Raghav thought.

There was a whole bunch of people rushing towards him. He

stood on a bench to see the group behind it and was terrified and euphoric at the same time. "The damn queue" Raghav shouted, "is the longest I have ever seen."

"What are you saying, I can't hear anything." Vik yelled.

"Nothing." Raghav shouted again.

There were people, people and more people as far as his eyes could see and the worst or perhaps the best part- they were increasing both in number and enthusiasm for entry. 'But how do I let all of them in together, there isn't enough place to accommodate them' he wondered.

He looked upto the sky. 'God you are great, this is excellent.'

Then suddenly something ran through his mind. He looked at Vik and Nirvaan – two tall people who were his makeshift bouncers for the evening, allowing people entry only when Raghav signalled.

"Guys," Raghav screamed, "charge five hundred bucks per person for entry, that's the only way to reduce this chaos."

"Did you say five hundred?" Nirvaan shrieked.

"Yeah."

And as soon as he said that, people turned to their wallets.

"Here's thousand bucks for the two of us." yelled two youngsters as they begged for entry.

"Here two grand, please allow the four of us to enter, please." another one begged.

"We've been waiting for an hour, here's the money, come on let us in now." two girls yelled this time.

'Wow.. wow.. wow..' Raghav was ecstatic. He had not thought of charging any entry fee, but the situation demanded it. And it was still working, bloody well working.

'This is excellent' he thought 'this is doing better business that I ever imagined and right from day one.' He looked up at the sky again to thank his stars.

An hour passed that way and this time Raghav had other problems. The money – it was flooding from everywhere. A mere five hundred rupee, it appeared, was nothing with respect to what it had to offer. A doubt hovered in Raghav's mind whether he should raise that to a thousand bucks.

'Oh no' he thought 'greed isn't good.'

"Raghav let me go inside now." Nirvaan yelled amongst a plethora of other voices. "I'm bored here."

"Shut up asshole, stay where you are." Raghav commanded.

A few minutes later Raghav went for a peek inside his club. The place was packed. There wasn't an iota of space unoccupied. 'God it's full and bustling.' The atmosphere was electrifying. The air was filled with insurmountable energy. The excitement around sent tremors down his spine. It took some time for the reality to sink inside. He could already see his place boasting of couples. The two guys who were the first ones to fish out the thousand bucks were already with their respective girls. "Wow!" Raghav sounded grateful, "this is exactly what I had planned."

People yelled and screamed and enjoyed every bit of it. Food and drinks sold like hot cakes as people feasted on the low prices. A hundred bucks for a chicken tikka and a beer was an unparalleled price in a pub.

"Marvellous" Raghav punched his fist in the air. "This is it, this is exactly what I wanted."

He wobbled on his toes and meandered through the people to find a way out. When he was out, there was a frenzied crowd waiting for him.

"Please let us in." was all he could gather from the feisty crowd. There were screams, squeals, shouts, yelling and all sorts of noise for an entry.

Finally Raghav announced, "Alright people listen, the place is full, I can't let any more of you guys in, please understand, I'll see you all tomorrow."

The crowd erupted disconsolately but finally co-operated and dispersed. Raghav let out a breath of relief and glanced beatifically at Vik and Nirvaan.

At his smile, Nirvaan protested "now what, at least now let me go inside."

"Buzz off, enjoy yourself." Raghav roared.

There was finally silence outside with only the muffled sound from inside. Raghav wore a satisfied look. Suddenly he started laughing. Vik followed suit.

"Didn't I tell you Vik, this was meant to be a success."

"Success yes, but to this limit."

"Can you believe it, I have made close to fifty grand in the last hour only on the entry fee."

Vik was still laughing.

"And I have not yet checked how much I earned through coffee two hours back."

Two hours back when D'CoBo Club was inaugurated, the aroma of coffee had stung passersby as they dropped in and were then spell bound by the wide variety of coffee, sandwiches, cookies, brownies and pastries at relatively low prices. Raghav knew at once just the coffee part of it would do good business.

An old man confessed, "This is the best and cheapest coffee I have ever had."

"Wow." Raghav chuckled.

As the evening passed and darkness crept in, the average age inside D'CoBo Club kept on decreasing. At nine sharp, Raghav with the help of his few workers quickly transposed the place into a pub. And it was then that the longest and widest queue Raghav had ever seen started forming.

"Oh my god, people, people and more people."

"Wow, wow, wow, wow......" he was screaming and suddenly he woke up to his own voice. The crowd was gone, the screams disappeared. For an instant, he couldn't muster what had happened. He called Vik, and Nirvaan. No answer.

As awareness dawned, the smile left his face.

"Oh my God!" Raghav shrieked, "This was a dream, just a bloody dream, God no."

He looked at his watch. 7:10 AM.

"Oh god so this really was a dream."

He rubbed his eyes, scratched his head and yawned hopelessly. "But aren't early morning dreams supposed to be true?" It was neither a question nor an answer. And he didn't bother to think about that either. He was sure even if it wasn't, this dream would be a reality.

Shunning his thoughts, he threw away his blanket and shot up from his bed to get ready for office. He was confident that these were surely the last few days of this monotonous and drudgery job from 8:00 am to 8:00 pm. And yes, no more boss.

In his office he could hardly concentrate as he slouched on his chair, daydreaming. 'Day after tomorrow then' he thought 'so this is it, I have finally come that close.'

"Excellent!" he shrieked. His voice was much louder and high pitched than he wanted it to be and it turned a few heads towards him. "Sorry guys, carry on." he apologized. He looked at his watch. "58 hours to go, damn!." This was the hardest wait ever. All the last seven years flashed before him. The endless days, and nights of hard work; that day when he got the idea when he was drunk, his rendezvous with Nirvaan who further ameliorated his plan and then more hard work. He knew he really deserved a success. It would be fantastic, he thought, if things went exactly as they did in his dream. Or even a fraction less would be alright. But only a small fraction.

His phone rang. He didn't bother picking it up. "Must be that shithead boss, screw him." He looked around, everyone appeared busy or so it appeared. He looked at his watch "57 hours to go, still! Oh god" he screamed again. And then again he apologized when the heads turned towards him.

"I have to find a way to kill time now." he uttered to himself. He took out a piece of paper and started writing numbers from one to hundred. It took him only six minutes to do that. Frustrated, he continued the counting in roman numerals. Eleven minutes passed. "Uhh.. god what is the matter, why is this damn time not passing."

He repeated the counting again this time in letters. "One, two, three...., ninety eight, ninety nine, hundred." Twenty three minutes passed. "What the hell" he screamed but this time managed to keep his voice down. He sauntered towards the loo.

He found the washroom very different or perhaps it was the first time he actually noticed it. There was a huge mirror above the wash basin neatly trimmed at its edges. He applied water to his hair and dressed it. Then changed it to a new hair style. And then again changed it. He didn't bother looking at his watch. The little alleyway that led to the loo had got small flower pots along one side. Raghav found himself staring at them. He bent down to have a close look at the little plants. They appeared beautiful. He brushed his fingers against them. He noticed them for a few more minutes, and then left the loo. In all, seventeen minutes passed.

When he returned to his desk, he took out a novel from his drawer. He normally always kept a novel there to read in his free time. He read two pages, and then threw it away. Frustrated, he scrambled out for a smoke.

Finally evening came and it brought a smile on Raghav's face. He went straight to Vik's house. Vik's mother opened the door and greeted him.

"Where's Vik aunty?"

"Where else can he be? In his room of course, sleeping." the anger in her voice had receded and given way to hatred and frustration.

"Sleeping now, eight in the evening."

Raghav rushed towards Vik's room and threw his shoes at him.

"Wake up you moron."

"Who is that?" Vik answered peeping through his blanket.

"Raghav, what are you doing now so early in the morning?"

"Ass it's eight in the evening not in the morning."

"Oh is it?" Vik got up rubbing his eyes and checked his watch. "Oh shit you are right." He stretched himself as though he had been working all day "what happened?" he asked in a pesky voice.

"I should be asking that." Raghav said "you sleeping at this time?"

"Yeah I remember now." Vik answered yawning, "I was so bored in the morning that I started drinking and then I guess I passed out without having lunch. God no wonder my stomach is growling, I'm so hungry. Hey mom get me some food." he shouted.

"You lazy bastard, anyway I've something interesting to tell you."

"Yeah tell me." Vik yawned again.

And Raghav began, "I had this wonderful dream today Vik, about the first day of D'CoBo Club. All I could see was people and more people. So much so that we were charging five hundred bucks for entry per person to manage the crowd, can you believe that?"

"No." Vik replied curtly.

"Yeah seriously five hundred man I was just thinking can't we actually do that."

Vik thought for a second. "Yeah we can try."

"I'm sure no guy would mind paying it."

"Think so." Vik approved.

"And perhaps I would charge only the guys, not girls, can't be restricting their entry, isn't it?"

"Perfect Raghav, don't even think about it anymore, just perfect, now get out and let me sleep."

Raghav sighed "sleep again." Tired and exhausted himself, he lay next to him. "Alright do whatever, I'm going to Priya Complex tomorrow at ten in the morning for the final check, I want you to come along with me, be ready at half past nine, I'll pick you up."

"You crazy?" Vik declined "I get up at noon."

Raghav kicked his butt hard. "Sharp 09:30 am."

He checked his watch "48 hours to go." Then he took his diary out and went through his pending list – learn flying, learn horse riding, vacation to Bahamas. There were far too many. He had been too busy to take out time for them over the last few years, though he did manage to complete a few.

'Time has come to knock these out of my diary.' He thought.

"Hey Vik, how about a holiday in Bahamas next month."

Vik turned around to face him and smiled, "you are something dude."

"Why... what?" Raghav sort of complained.

"Well at least finish one thing before jumping in to another."

"No seriously Vik." Raghav said, "I can see the future clearly, I'll be earning big bucks through my club and following all my passions religiously from now on."

Vik was still smiling.

"A holiday in Bahamas would be followed by learning horse riding and then flying and then...."

Vik observed him precisely. Raghav wasn't speaking to him. But to himself. All these years due to the austerity with which he had been living to achieve this one goal were finally coming out. Lying over his bed, half awake, Vik prayed 'oh dear god, please fulfil all dreams of my best friend.'

Raghav was still speaking when Vik finished his little prayer. He looked at him with fondness. Finally when Raghav was done, Vik quipped "you are too excited about life, aren't you?"

19

'DRINK TILL YOU DROP'

Sharp half past nine, Raghav was outside Vik's house. He rang the door bell. "Where's Vik aunty" he asked as soon as the door opened.

"Where else?" Vik's mother replied.

Raghav rushed towards Vik's room, thrilled and excited about the day. All the excitement vanished as he opened the door.

"Oh God you are still sleeping?" Raghav yelled, "wake up you moron."

He pulled Vik's legs and dropped him on the floor, then dragged him towards the bathroom.

"What are you up to Raghav?" Vik cried.

"You have twenty minutes to get ready."

Twenty minutes later Raghav pulled Vik out of the house.

"Let me have breakfast at least." Vik pleaded.

"You are too late for that."

They reached Priya Complex fifteen minutes past ten. It was a bright sunny day, the heat of the sun juxtaposed with the cool wind that blew from north. It made the weather pleasant.

When they were outside D'CoBo Club, Vik screamed "Hey what is that?" He was looking at two huge boards placed outside the club, one on each side. It read in huge block letters:

'DRINK TILL YOU DROP'

DRINKS ON THE HOUSE FOR THE FIRST HUNDRED.

"Hey that's nice." Vik adjusted his tone to a more approving one as he comprehended the idea. "Very nice indeed."

"Isn't it?" Raghav said "I want a bloody stampede out here tomorrow, similar to the one in my dream. People should fight and vie with each other to be in the first hundred."

"You are a slimy bastard Raghav." Vik teased "You know well how to entice people, huh."

"That's business my friend."

They laughed as they entered the club. Inside there were two huge rooms – the first rectangular and the second circular that was even bigger. The first room had a seating arrangement on one side that could accommodate at least fifty people. The furniture was judiciously chosen by Raghav to serve the purpose both in the day and night for coffee and alcohol respectively. It shouldn't look odd to the coffee goers and boozers alike, he had planned. The other side of the rectangular room was occupied by a bar that spanned the entire length of the room. Again Raghav was very careful about its appearance because the same place would also serve coffee during the daytime. He had concentrated more on the coffee part of it as that was during the light hours. As for the bar, he knew he could always put dim lights overhead warding off the possibility of a close-up survey by the boozers. He was, however, a bit discontent about the same.

The next room was almost circular. All along its periphery were little book shelves full of books of all types. Raghav himself was fond of reading while drinking coffee, hence he included the idea. There was a brass rod that penetrated the centre of each shelf and Vik noticed the book shelves were not even touching the floor. As he pushed it from one side, it started rotating, pivoting about the rod and easily turned towards the other side. Vik found it to be an innovative and relatively simple idea. "So you don't want these book shelves to be visible during the night, huh." he asked. There was a shade of appreciation in his tone.

"God you are smart" Raghav snapped "Actually it serves another purpose." He pushed the shelf till it faced the other side. "Do you see these?" Raghav pointed to small apertures in the wood. "These would do the job of allowing coloured streaks of light to pass through these little projectors fitted aft of the shelves." Vik stretched to look at the projectors behind.

"The coloured streaks of light passing through" Raghav added, "would add a sensational effect to the aura of this place at night."

"Right." Vik agreed.

In the centre of the room were mobile chairs and tables in case the seating arrangement fell short during the coffee hours in the rectangular room. They would be removed as the circular floor did the job of a mini dance floor in the night. Raghav didn't make much of an arrangement for the disc lights overhead as the roof was high enough for them to look odd.

"So Vik how do you find the setup, satisfied." Raghav raised his brow.

"Quite satisfied actually," Vik replied with a wide grin, "you have done a decent job I must say."

"Decent." Raghav condemned vociferously, "It's an awesome job I have done." His eyes bored deeply into Vik's, challenging them.

Vik shuddered, "That's exactly what I meant, sorry wrong use of the word."

"No, not really." Raghav said factiously, "There are some areas where there is a scope for improvement, for example look at that bar that's not come up well, not upto my expectations."

Vik nodded.

"But anyway, I'll get the place revamped when money pours into my account."

"So for now be satisfied with this." Vik advised.

"Yeah I pretty much am."

For the next hour, they hung around inside. Raghav was guiding his workers meticulously as they scrambled about their job. The layout of the place had been planned well in advance by Raghav and he ensured it was the exact replica of the one in his mind. He had also decided the transformation he would bring about after a few months if he could rake in some money. A lot of money.

"Shall we leave Vik or do you have any comments or suggestions?"

"None, it all looks good, let's go."

As they came out, Raghav remembered something. "Hey did I tell you about my school band that will be performing live the day after tomorrow."

Vik tried remembering hard. "No you didn't." he replied hesitantly.

"Of course I did tell you about 'The Mavericks', they are the coolest rock band in town." He took out his phone and dialled a number.

"Hello," a voice said.

"Hello Tejas, Raghav here. All set for Saturday."

"Sure we'll be there."

"Right seven sharp I want you guys here, take care." he hung up.

"So we have a rock performance as well" Vik said.

"Yes of course, the rock culture is growing up here, thought could entertain the crowd with a bit of that as well and trust me this band is quite famous amongst the youth."

"But I didn't see a rock performance advertised in your banners anywhere." Vik asked "or did I?"

"No you didn't, I have done that on purpose, want to give the crowd a surprise."

"Well I hope they don't get too surprised." Vik winked.

Raghav kicked him hard "don't give me those kinky looks, anyway I'll see you again in the evening, have called all others at Mocha for a coffee treat."

"A coffee treat." Vik found himself intrigued by that.

"Well I want to formally invite them tomorrow for the most important day of my life." Raghav's eyes gleamed with happiness when he said that "and especially the girls are to be warned to be on time at least tomorrow" a slight frown bordered around his face.

"And what about me, you haven't invited me formally yet." Vik asked and wondered a second later what a stupid question to ask.

Raghav stared at him ominously for a few seconds. The slap Vik got then was the hardest he had ever got in his life.

A minute's walk and they reached the car parking. The metallic Blue Swift roared to life as Raghav supplied the ignition. When he pulled his car out of the parking, he ran his eyes through the entire complex. The memories flooded his mind in a flash. This was the place he called his second home. The place he boozed, partied, celebrated, analyzed, planned and surveyed. And this was the same place he wished to rule. A gift for his fellow visitors, he thought.

"So its fixed for tomorrow then, my dear Priya complex, when you would be boasting of my name day and night."

He saluted and sped away.

20
LIFE? FUTURE? PLANS?

The stage was all set, the preparation were all done. D'CoBo club was all primed to kick start the next day. Raghav's happiness knew no bounds. His excitement was at its peak, if it increased he would definitely have needed a doctor. When he reached home in the afternoon after dropping Vik, he sat on a chair and stared at the wall clock almost relentlessly. The wait for the evening felt like an eternity. He did not have lunch or water. He didn't sleep, read. He didn'watch television. He waited.

Finally when evening came, he was exultant. "Time to see my friends." he uttered. 'Well atleast the next two hours would pass easily', he thought. *And then it would be just the night and day tomorrow separating me from my seven year long dream.* His heart was beating faster, adrenaline surging through his veins as he staggered around. He was excited, he was exhilarated.

Mocha was a dimly lit coffee house in the heart of Defence Colony Market. After the recent ruckus of commercializing the residential areas, Mocha had shifted from M block market in Greater Kailash. It was famous for its traditional hookahs offered in various flavours and a trancelike aura that prevailed. People lazed around enjoying coffee and a smoke.

When Raghav entered Mocha he remembered its tagline – 'Coffee and Conversations'. Then he cast some light on D'CoBo club's tagline – 'Walk in single, walk out couple.'

"Oh mine's definitely better." He hopped and skipped and jumped when he said that.

"Hey guys," Raghav greeted Vik and Nirvaan "and oh my God you girls," he looked at Ruheen, Purnima and Rachna in bewilderment. "You girls on time, what happened? Is everything alright?" There was an edge of concern in his voice.

"What do you mean ?" Purnima protested, tucking her a few strands of hair beneath her ears. She had got a permanent hair straightening done recently and was boasting about it. "We were on time, look at your watch, you are an hour late."

"Alright Purnima that's so sweet of you guys."

"Thanks for your appreciation."

For the next half an hour it was only Raghav who spoke. No one had seen him as elated and excited as he was today. Not even Vik.

"Guys I won't get any sleep tonight, it's been at least seven years now since I told Vik about this dream of mine and he scoffed at me, and tomorrow the same dream is coming true.

"I didn't scoff at you." Vik interjected, "It was just that you told me about it in such a weird way, standing on your chair in a pub with people staring at you."

"Yeah yeah" Raghav laughed "I remember that." He remained silent for a few moments as he commemorated those days; how pissed off he had been with his work and life then, so much so that he had taken up drinking every day and the same drinking became the idea of his life. He had been in love with alcohol all the more since then, but he had restricted his drinking so that he could make a career of it.

"I hope guys this works." There was a note of yearning in his voice "People like my place specially the idea of dating, I have really worked hard."

"Of course it will Raghav." Ruheen asserted, "Hard work always pays, don't worry."

He nodded, "We'll see and you know what, it's just twenty two hours from now. Gosh I don't know what I will be doing tomorrow at this time."

"You'll be jumping in excitement! you will be on cloud nine Raghav. All of us are sure about that." Rachna said.

"Thanks, thanks guys for all the support." he acknowledged. He drank a glass of cold water, rubbed his hands and fluttered, "Alright time to delegate duties."

"Duties!" Purnima screamed biting her nails.

"Of course." Raghav replied "first of all, guys ensure that all of you are there at six sharp, the entry starts at seven and all three of you girls" he looked at them with his hands folded. "Please, please please be on time at least tomorrow."

"Don't worry Raghav," Vik interjected "I'll take care of that one. But what time will you be there?"

"Can't wait for the evening!" He smiled, "Alright so Vik and Nirvaan, both of you take the roles as in my dream, use your tall frame be my bouncers for tomorrow but outside."

"Outside," Nirvaan protested, "But all the girls will be inside." and immediately he knew he had made a *fause pas. Shit what an idiot I am.* He didn't dare looking at Ruheen. "Alright done, I'll be outside" he shouted, "I don't care about the damn girls. Let them be inside, bloody bitches."

Raghav laughed, "Sensible boy Nirvaan, alright." he turned to face Rachna "In keeping with your penchant for alcohol, you be at the bar guiding the bartenders. Offer free drinks to the first hundred, they'll be showing you a pass."

"Thanks Raghav." Rachna looked happy. *I'll be at the bar, vow.*

Raghav observed her excitement, "Hey, hey, hey wait a minute, don't get any wrong ideas, you don't drink tomorrow, please."

"Yeah of course Raghav," she replied still smiling, "would have just a few."

"Less than a few." Raghav amended.

"Okay."

"God all you people are great, anyway, moving on to Purnima and Ruheen, I think both of you should be inside making use of your conversation skills and ensure that no one inside gets bored, of course if the music allows that."

"Alrighteeeeee....e" both of them loved this job.

"And what about you Raghav, what are you going to do? Sleep is it?" Vik inquired.

"Oh no ....o ....o I'll be the one counting the money, it's going to be flowing tomorrow you see."

"I hope so."

They howled, laughed, sang and screamed the next hour. Raghav's voice was the loudest amongst the six of them.

"Wow Raghav, you look so excited." Purnima grinned. "I wish I could be as much excited as you are sometime in my life."

"Sure you'll be when any of your future plans in life is realized."

"Life? Future? Plans? What are you talking about?" Purnima asked in awe. "You don't make plans, things just happen."

"No Pooh you are mistaken." Raghav corrected, "Things don't just happen, you make them happen."

"Alright buddy," Vik intervened, "please none of your philosophical shit today, I'm in no mood, let's celebrate for tomorrow."

Raghav nodded "As you say sir."

The coffee was done along with a few snacks. The evening was to begin at seven the next day. It was decided that all of them would be there at six in case of any last minute goof ups.

Raghav was thrilled. Twenty one hours were left. He took his diary out and kissed it. "Guys I think you should all get a diary, it really helps."

21
THE D-DAY !!!

"God what's with these girls," Vik blurted "always."

Vik and Nirvaan had been outside their house half an hour back, honking and waiting but in vain. Nirvaan could see Vik had lost his patience. "Easy my boy, this is nothing, you'll get used to it."

"Yeah right but look at the time, it's already half past five, how on earth would we reach Priya by six now?" the anger in Vik's voice had risen in proportion with passing time. "Raghav would already be there waiting for us and this is when he had warned these girls yesterday to be on time."

"God Vik chill." Nirvaan tried appeasing him with a cigarette. "You know on an average, I have waited at least forty five minutes for Ruheen and this is slightly better than my all time average wait of an hour with all the other girls."

Vik didn't answer. His face became red with anger.

"This is still thirty minutes dude, relax, think about all the good things in life, take a deep breath and accept the most bitter truth of life – girls can never be on time." Nirvaan clenched his teeth when he uttered the last sentence.

Vik could discern a shade of anger in his tone. "Okay." he replied lamely.

As Nirvaan had guessed rightly, a meeting was being held upstairs. It had begun a few hours back and was finally on the verge of completion. It was a big day for Raghav so the dressing had to be spot on. And the horde of guys that would be present warranted a right decision and selection of clothes. After three rounds of rejection, they finally made up their mind on what to wear for the evening.

Nirvaan was the first to see them coming down the stairs "hey look Vik, the girls have come."

"Don't you guys think you are a bit late?" Vik asked as politely as he could when the girls settled door inside the car.

"Yeah maybe." Purnima retorted, "But just a few minutes here and there is alright Vik, come on."

Just a few minutes!

Having said that, Purnima wasn't still content. Something was bothering her. "Hey guys don't you feel the neck is a bit deep."

"Very deep actually." Vik replied.

"Oh no," she shouted, "see girls wasn't I telling you? Wait Vik I'll just change and come."

Vik clenched his fists and in a flash the car sped off. "Sorry baby if it wasn't for Raghav, I would have allowed that."

In a few minutes they were on Ring Road after crossing the Defence Colony Market. Vik checked his watch. It was a quarter to six. "Shit!" he snorted, "we are running damn late, Raghav will kill us."

"Easy Vik." Nirvaan advised, "We'll be there in half an hour"

"I know but I promised Raghav to be there by six."

"Oh never mind Vik." Purnima bellowed from behind. "Haste makes waste, just drive safe. I don't want any accidents."

Vik however ignored her advice and drove the car in a frenzied rush, zigzagging through cars, buses and two wheelers using the brake and accelerator deftly. Ten minutes to six and they had crossed the AIIMS flyover.

"Ah this was the toughest part." Vik breathed. "Coming out from South Extension towards AIIMS, now it's going to be a merry ride."

"Certainly." Nirvaan acknowledged.

But as soon as he said that he ran into a chastic situation when he least wanted it. Vik found himself in the centre of a colossal traffic jam that stretched from the AIIMS flyover to Dhaula Kuan. There was a deafening noise of horns from vehicles along with an enormous chaos as people vied to move ahead. Drivers honked almost continuously urging the ones in front to move. But it was all in vain. The traffic was almost stuck and moved at a snail's pace. Vik grew unsettled at his seat and so did others. "Shit Shit, I told you guys be on time, now see we are trapped, there's no way we are getting out of this mess." he growled.

The girls were quiet.

"Hey relax Vik." Nirvaan suggested, "Let's go out and check out the problem."

They came back after ten minutes.

"Oh god there is an accident," Vik returned yelling, "God we are stuck."

"Where, what happened?" Ruheen asked. There was a worried air about her.

"Just a hundred metres to our left." Vik replied, "Rescue work is on, they are taking the patient to AIIMS."

"Oh that's sad." Purnima said as she shook her head. "There are so many of these accidents in Delhi, it's such a shame."

"Guys," she continued when Vik and Nirvaan settled down on their respective seats, "did you manage to have a look at that unfortunate person, maybe he needs some help."

"Damn him and damn you Purnima." Vik castigated "There's no time for all that shit. It's ten minutes past six already, my friend would be waiting desperately for all of us on his most important day, let's just get out of here."

Ten minutes later, the traffic situation improved as Vik snaked past the cars. He took a left before Hyatt towards the outer Ring Road. It was already twenty minutes past six.

"God can you guys believe it's barely forty minutes before the inauguration and we still haven't reached!" Vik hollered.

No one said a word. All of them felt miserable and wretched. Vik drove at a breakneck speed for the last part of the journey. They were finally there at half past six.

"Run, lets run guys." Vik ordered everybody as soon as he parked the car. "And girls don't even dare to look at the mirror, you are all looking stunning, now come on."

They entered the complex from behind Priya. Everyone had kept their fingers crossed. "Guys," Vik said, "I hope to see a damn queue outside D'CoBo club as Raghav had dreamed."

"Oh I'm sure of that." Nirvaan replied.

All around them they saw posters and banners of Raghav's club. They boasted the tagline "Drink till you drop" and "Walk in single, walk out couple."

"Oh I wish I see a stampede here." Vik said in an exhilarated tone. And when they took a left turn from Priya Cinema towards D'CoBo club, Vik jumped with excitement. And so did others.

"Hey guys look over there, just look that side, I can see a huge crowd before our club." Vik was jumping like a madman.

"Oh yeah that's great!" Rachna bawled. "Oh God Raghav will be so happy."

"You bet!" Nirvaan bellowed "This is awesome man. There's a huge rush, wow."

They sprinted towards the club holding each other's hands.

"Oh God where is Raghav." Vik thundered. "I feel like hugging, kissing and congratulating him. This is exactly what he wanted, a god damn stampede."

"Oh I wonder how Raghav would be feeling." Purnima screamed. "He'll be so happieeeeeee." The last word was stretched for more than five seconds.

They finally reached the outer fringes of the crowd. As they tried to traverse through the raucous bunch of people, they found themselves pushed behind.

"Oh hell, how are we going to get inside this?" Purnima squealed. "This will spoil my dress."

"Wait wait." Vik was shouting. "let's try again."

They all came outside and ran a few metres to get a bit of a momentum to rush through the crowd. But it was all in vain. They were all pushed aside again.

"Damn," Ruheen shouted this time, "this is crazy, people have gone absolutely insane."

"What is that?" Rachna hollered. "I can't hear anything."

The fact was that no one could hear anything. The crowd had gone berserk as in Raghav's dreams. All of them wanted to be in the first hundred. D'CoBo club had been advertised so widely that all the youth of Delhi was aware of it.

"We've to find a way out of this Vik." Nirvaan said, "We can't be waiting like this forever, Raghav would be waiting for us inside, come on think of something."

Vik took out his phone and called Raghav, "Wait let me call him up and at least tell him that we are here, let him organize something."

"God," he cried a minute later, "he's not even picking up his phone."

"I bet he's angry with us."

Vik knew Nirvaan could be right, "Alright never mind, let's find a way through this then."

They went behind a few metres so that they could be audible.

"Alright guys listen." Vik ordered, "We have to again try and get inside, let's repeat what we did last time."

Again they ran with full force and brutality but were pushed back yet again by the people in front. "Hey you tough guys," Nirvaan condemned, "we are the friends of the owner of this place, come on let us pass."

"Oh yeah," one of the tough guys smirked, "tell you what I am the father of the owner of this place, now what."

"Bloody jerk" Purnima dismissed, "no bloody manners, huh".

They again came back a few metres back to plan their entry.

"Alright folks" Rachna took charge this time. "I'll be leading, followed by Ruheen and Purnima and then you guys follow, you guys are anyway good for nothing."

"Alright," Vik agreed. He looked at his watch. It was just twenty five minutes to the inauguration. "Come on Rachna let's rush."

And the plan was executed fairly well. Rachna used her tough body to a marvellous effect pushing past the crowd and the others followed. Within five minutes they were at the gate. "Thank God we are safe." Purnima exclaimed, "this was the most terrifying moment of my life."

"Alright where's Raghav now?" Vik sputtered as he looked around hastily.

"Oh don't even bother," Ruheen suggested "he'll be in the loo shitting in his pants with excitement."

Vik nodded. He asked the bouncers.

"Sir must be inside." replied one of them in a husky voice. He was a few inches taller than six feet with broad shoulders and bulging biceps.

'Wonder what's with Raghav' Nirvaan thought 'when he's got such giants as bouncers why does he need me and Vik for this job, I better go inside.'

"Hey come on guys let's go in and congratulate Raghav, I am dying to see the expression on his face." Vik bustled with excitement.

"Right." they said following him.

Inside everything was set. The club was waiting to be inaugurated. The bartenders and waiters had assumed their respective positions. Even the 'Mavericks' – the band that were performing tonight had arrived. They were on a makeshift stage at the far end of the second room doing their last bit of rehearsal.

"Hey there's the bar." Rachna freaked out "that's my place for the evening."

"Relax Rachna," Ruheen said, "make sure you don't drink it all."

"Oh don't worry about that." Rachna smiled as she trotted towards the bar.

"Where is this Raghav?" Nirvaan asked "It's just twenty minutes before the inauguration."

"That's exactly what I am wondering," Vik replied, "wait let's ask these guys." He pointed towards the members of the band.

"Hey you guys seen Raghav?" Vik asked in a loud voice to counteract the sound of electric guitar and drums.

"Nopes we are looking for him ourselves." a tall man replied through shoulder length hair that shrouded his entire face. His hair was so dark and dense, Vik couldn't even see his lips when they moved.

"How can you see him," Vik said "you can't even see me hairy boy."

"What?" asked the hairy boy with umpteen disgust.

"Oh never mind, I'll find him, you carry on."

"I think Ruheen is right, he must be in the washroom." Nirvaan suggested.

"Yeah, I think as much." Vik replied.

He wasn't there.

"Damn what's with Raghav?" Vik sniffed "Nirvaan ask those bartenders and waiters' maybe they know."

They didn't know.

"God this is strange, nobody knows where Raghav is." Vik went back outside. The crowd and their roar had increased. They were begging for entry. Vik checked his watch, it was still ten minutes to seven.

"Hey guys," Vik told the bouncers "don't allow any of them inside till I figure out where Raghav is."

"Right sir." one of the huge man replied.

Vik tried Raghav's number. He didn't pick up. "Damn you Raghav." Vik snapped his phone.

He ran his eyes through the crowd. They were on their feet, screaming and shouting and had gone absolutely berserk. There was only one thing Vik could decipher – they would have killed for an entry in D'CoBo club.

'Wow, Raghav would love this, his dream has come true.' He mused 'but where on earth is he?'

Just then he got a call.

It was from AIIMS.

22

WHEN LIFE TRICKED ME…

Twenty five minutes later, Vik, Nirvaan, Ruheen, Rachna and Purnima were streaming along the long corridor of AIIMS hospital.

"Where is he?" Vik yelled at the receptionist. "Raghav, Raghav Arora"

"Room 301."

They sprinted towards his room. Usually the aura of a hospital and whiff of medicines associated with it triggered a wave of nausea in Vik, but today he was panting and so disoriented that he felt nothing. He wiped his tears with the sleeves of his shirt. "Guys find room 301, fast." he shouted.

As they entered the room, a spate of queasiness flooded them. They couldn't believe what they saw. The sight presented to them sent tremors down their spine. Raghav's face was smashed and the skin of his face was burnt. It exposed his cheekbones and jaw. He had suffered third degree burns almost all over his body. His burnt clothes were stuck to his skin and soaked in his blood. Oxygen was being administered to him and intravenous fluids supplied through injections that pierced his hands.

"Oh my God, oh my God!" Vik screamed in horror. "What the hell happened, what happened to Raghav?"

He rushed towards him but the doctor stopped him midway. "Please control yourself, he is unconscious." the doctor said.

"Unconscious! what are you saying" he howled, "Hey Nirvaan what is he talking about?"

Nirvaan took a deep breath, "Relax Vik, he'll be alright, nothing is going to happen to him."

"Nothing is going to happen to him," Vik sniffed with contempt "what's wrong with you guys? What are you saying? He's absolutely fine, come on let's take him, people are waiting for entry in his club." He broke into a paroxysm of sobs "People are waiting for entry, it is the most important day of his life." He fell on the floor and sobbed uncontrollably. "It's the most important day of his life doctor, please do something, please."

The sudden shock unleashed a spasm of tears in Purnima and Ruheen as Nirvaan and Rachna watched in despair. Tears escaped their moist eyes as they found it hard to suppress them.

"But doctor what happened to him?" Nirvaan whimpered shedding tears.

"Accident." the doctor replied, "He met with a terrible accident this evening."

"He continued, "Just after the AIIMS flyover, a drunken driver smashed into Raghav's car from left. The sudden impact triggered an explosion within a fraction of a second as the other car was was being seen by CNG." The doctor shook his head. "It was very unfortunate, the driver died on the spot but we somehow managed to bring your friend here. However," the doctor tried his best to convey his last statement euphemistically "I fear it's a bit too late."

"Late?" Vik screamed as he got up from the floor. "I don't care doctor you bloody well save him and now, right now, he has to be in the club, people are waiting for him, you get it."

"Vik control yourself please," Nirvaan tried pacifying him.

Suddenly Vik stopped crying. "Accident, hey doctor what did you just say accident, where? After the AIIMS flyover."

"Yeah right." the doctor nodded.

"Oh my God!" Vik screamed, "It was him, it was Raghav over there, he was the one in the accident, oh God, no."

"You asshole Vik," Purnima punched him from behind, "Didn't I tell you to have a look at the unfortunate person, maybe he needs some help but you yelled back at me, all this has happened because of you."

'Damn him and damn you Purnima, there's no time for this.' Vik remembered his words.

"Oh no, what have I done." Vik cried fervently as he found it hard to breathe. He walked towards the wall and smashed his head on it continuously as blood oozed through it.

"Vik stop, stop it man, what are you doing?" Nirvaan pulled him from behind "It's not your mistake."

"Of course it's my goddamn mistake, Raghav was just a hundred metres from us and I drove past him, shit no, Purnima told me to have a look at the guy, but damn me I didn't. I'm useless, good for nothing, Raghav has always been right in criticizing me." He started smashing his head again.

"Alright Vik enough, just stop." Nirvaan commanded. "It's everybody's mistake, don't worry, Raghav will be fine."

The doctor however had a sceptic look. Vik looked at his watch. It was quarter to eight, "Oh god this is so unreal, look at the time, it's already forty five minutes past the inauguration time. Raghav is losing his dream, the people will be waiting." He sprang towards the bed "Hey get up Raghav, come on get up, you can't just sleep like that, you are not me, I am supposed to do things like that, this is your dream Raghav, it has come true, your seven year long dream. Raghav, get up." he fell on the floor next to his bed and sobbed loudly, "Get up Raghav, please get up, you are not me."

Nirvaan emerged from behind wiping his own tears. He patted Vik's back, "Vik I suggest you go there and organize everything. Can't let the people wait, that will shalter his dream, we are all here to take care of him."

"No of course not." Vik rejected it firmly. "The club won't open unless he is there, it is his dream after all, he'll be okay in half an hour's time."

Vik cried hard. He had never expected this to happen. On his most important day, Raghav was on the death bed fighting for his life. He felt horrible. He looked at his friends. They were equally petrified and sad. "Why did it happen to him?" Vik asked facing his friends, "He is the most sincere and disciplined guy amongst us, the most hard working person I've ever known, I should have been in his place, damn it." He slapped himself, "I'm anyway a useless moron, this world does not need me, I should have been there." He continued slapping himself and crying.

"Hey relax Vik, come on relax, he'll be fine, have faith." Nirvaan said as he looked up at the girls.

The girls looked totally woebegone. The sight of Raghav, their mentor and best friend, frightened the living daylight out of them. "Yeah seriously," Ruheen broke out "why did it happen to him? It should have happened to any one of us, not him." she sobbed.

Nirvaan came forward offering her a shoulder to cry on.

"Stay away Nirvaan, just leave me alone" she shouted.

"What has happened God? What has happened to us?" Purnima groaned, "It was all so perfect an hour back, the long queue, the people, the rampage, it was all so perfect. Raghav please get up, please get up, we all love you."

Half past eight. Raghav finally opened his eyes but the ominous sigh of the doctor suggested it wasn't for long.

"Oh God Raghav what happened?" Vik shrieked "Come on your club is waiting for you, don't screw it up. This is the most important day of your life, come on get up."

Raghav looked at Vik through half open eyes and then his other friends as though he didn't recognize them. He looked pale and exhausted.

"I'll miss you guys." he uttered and it appeared he said it with great pain and difficulty. His upper lip was smeared with blood and the lower lip trembled with pain.

"Oh no Raghav please don't say that," Vik screamed, "you'll be fine. Really, nothing is going to happen to you."

"Yeah Raghav, Vik is right." Ruheen added shrieking, "You know your club is a success. People are dying for an entry, your dream has come true Raghav, you have won."

Tears rolled down Raghav's eyes as he winced in pain. "Oh I wish I could see that." he cried.

"You'll see it Raghav, you'll surely see it." Vik said.

Raghav took Vik's hand in his. "I know one of these day's you'll do something big."

Vik nodded.

Raghav started breathing heavily. Suddenly everything became hazy.

"Oh I wish Vik" he said as he mustered all his energy. He was finding it difficult to speak. "I wish I had started pursuing my dream a day earlier, at least I could have seen how it fared, I guess I was late." He lifted his hands in mid air and gestured towards his friends. They all came closer. "Life is short, really short, didn't I tell you guys." Raghav said with a slur.

And then his eyes closed.

Those were his last words.

Vik was devastated. "That was my best friend, my life, my mentor, he meant everything to me" he burst out crying. All the others burst into tears as well. They felt a palpable loss.

Vik broke into a paroxysm of weeping. The whole world shook around him. He wasn't that sad even when his father had died. "God why did it happen to you?" he wept. "He always told me life is short, don't waste it, work on your dreams and I always made fun of him, never listened to him. Today he died trying to explain that to me , I'm an idiot, I hate myself."

"Vik come on, it's not your fault please." Nirvaan said.

"No all this has happened because of me. He told me God will teach me a lesson one day and see what has happened now."

Vik cursed himself. "Sorry my friend, you were right. Life is short, I wished I had listened to you."

His eyes fell on a diary kept on the table next to the bed. He picked it up – 'Things to do before I die.'

"Oh God that's Raghav's diary." He kissed it. The top of it was slightly burnt. Vik opened and read through it.

"All those things he wanted to do he wrote them, so that once he achieved his dream, he could go on fulfilling them and today when that day came, look, look guys." he signalled towards Raghav's body "He's dead, life tricked him."

He continued brushing through the pages till he reached the last page - "My daily deeds", it said on top. There were three items under it:

1. Smile and be happy despite all hardships.

2. Respect the value of time.

There was a sudden rush of adrenaline in Vik's body as he found it hard to cope with it when he read the third line. It said:

3. Improve Vik's attitude towards life.

23

VIK'S BIG THING....

"One of these days I'll do something big." Vik said.

"Oh you mean none of these days don't you?" Raghav said.

Vik wiped his tears as he looked up at the sky. He was sitting on the terrace of his flat, holding Raghav's picture in his hand. "Oh I remember how I always made fun of Raghav, I'm so sorry my friend, please forgive me." He burst into tears. "I miss you dude, really miss you."

It had been two days since Raghav's death but it felt like a lifetime without him. Vik had been with him every day right after the first day when they had met in the pub. They had bonded big time because of their similar likes and dislikes except in their approach towards life. Vik wasn't even that close to his mother and sisters as he was to Raghav. It was an enormous loss.

Vik had been crying incessantly for the last two days. He didn't have food, drank minimal amount of water and didn't speak to anyone. His mother as always was peeved with his behaviour. "Have some food atleast Vik, and please accept the truth." His mother always pleaded.

But Vik turned down all her petitions. The truth pierced his heart and the pain was further aggravated as there was a part of him which took the responsibility of Raghav's death and there was another that gnawed at him whenever he thought of the mockery he made of Raghav's advice.

"What an idiot I am!" he cursed himself. "I always made fun of him." He kicked the concrete wall till his foot was bleeding. "I should have died not him." he wept bitterly.

He couldn't get rid of Raghav's voice and advice, they were all within him. 'Life is short Vik, really short, you have to be on your toes, if you want to achieve something in life.' He nodded "you were so right Raghav, life is actually so short."

Suddenly something ran through his mind. He got up in a flash and ran towards his room. He took a piece of paper and pen. On it he started writing things he thought he would do. But he would cancel them the very next moment he wrote them. Two hours passed that way and he couldn't figure out what he really wanted to do. "You were so right Raghav, you were so bloody right, I'm such a fool, I don't even know what I want to do and kept howling like an idiot that I would do a big thing someday."

He thought about Raghav. His dreams and clarity about life were poles apart from him, he knew that. 'But there must be something, I can do' he thought about it for another hour. It was in vain. His mother knocked on the door. "Vik please come out and have some food, how long are you going to do this to yourself?"

"I'm not hungry, just leave me alone." he shouted. He continued thinking, surveying his options. "Alright, I'm not going to move from here unless I decide what that big thing I want to do is." he promised himself.

"Shit, shit," he screamed half an hour later "what's wrong with me, I'm so screwed up, there's nothing, no such thing that I'll ever do."

He continued thinking. His brain had stopped working but he didn't give up. "I have to think about it and now."

Twenty minutes later, something clicked. He thought about it again. He took a sigh of relief a minute later. "This is it, this is what I'm going to do, my big thing."

He took out Raghav's diary from the shelf. "Yes Raghav, I'll do what you always wanted me to." He opened the yearly section. Under it he wrote something in big block letters.

"Yes Raghav I'll achieve my big thing within a year's time." he girded himself, then closed the diary.

But he wasn't satisfied still. His mind was still thinking. 'Something isn't right.' He opened the three monthly section. There he wrote something in it. He looked up at Raghav's picture on the wall, "This is for you my friend, my big thing in the next three months."

24

WHEN LOVE KICKED ME...

They were sitting at Barista in Vasant Vihar. Both of them were sad and distressed. They missed Raghav and his zeal for life.

Nirvaan looked at Ruheen. She looked beautiful. The round silver earrings accentuated her beauty. However she appeared lost. Nirvaan remembered the little story of the garden of roses that Raghav had told him when they were at Big Chill a few months back. He had scoffed at Raghav then, but suddenly he found sense in that. *She is the rose I have been looking out for, for so long.* He was convinced. He finally appeared to be sure of himself. 'Ruheen's going to be happy on hearing this', he thought.

"Ruheen I want to say something."

She didn't reply, only gave a slight nod.

"Well all these months, I have made you wait, I think that was a little harsh on my side."

"Really." The expression on her face was insouciant.

"Yeah I want to make it up to you for that."

Ruheen didn't reply. She wasn't exactly in the conversation.

"I think I'm sure about myself finally, I'm ready for a commitment."

Ruheen didn't answer.

"What happened Ruheen? You don't look happy, say something at least."

"You sure about yourself?" She asked with little interest.

"One hundred percent."

"But you know what Nirvaan? I am not."

"Wh ……. What?" He fumbled.

"Actually I am." she corrected herself.

Nirvaan took a breath of satisfaction. "You nearly got me there."

"Sure that I don't want to be with you anymore." She concluded her statement with a glacial look.

Nirvaan couldn't quite comprehend what she had said. For a moment he thought, she was joking.

"What are you saying?" He rejected with contempt.

"Yes Nirvaan I don't want to be with you."

Nirvaan laughed, "Are you insane? What has happened to you? I'm telling you that I'm ready for a commitment, then why are you acting so smart? Isn't that what you wanted?"

"Yes you are right." Ruheen nodded, "But you have taken a hell of a lot of time to decide that. I was an idiot to wait for you. I have decided to go back to Lucknow and teach those underprivileged children in the school that my father had started."

Nirvaan was still amused. "What are you saying?"

"Yes Nirvaan, I'm going back, I don't need you." She spoke outright. "Raghav was right, life is actually too short to be wasted and I have wasted more than a year on a pig like you. From now on I'll do what brings happiness to me and not just wait for happiness to knock my door."

Nirvaan stared at her blankly.

"And sorry to say Nirvaan," She continued, "waiting for you had been the worst time of my life." She stood up to leave.

"Hey wait Ruheen," Nirvaan pleaded, "at least listen to what I have to say."

"Good bye Nirvaan and please learn to be content in your life."

Nirvaan looked at her walking away from him. He couldn't believe what had just happened.

Suddenly he felt a piercing pain deep inside. He never expected Ruheen to walk out of his life like that. "I love you Ruheen, don't do this to me, please come back." he shouted.

Ruheen heard what he said but didn't stop.

He was too late.

25

THE LESSON LEARNT.....

Rachna lay on her bed distraught. Raghav's words echoed in her mind. "Life is short Rachna, really short." She looked at her watch. It was two in the morning but she couldn't sleep. Raghav's words didn't leave her.

"Rachna I thought you were hell bent on achieving your dream just like me."

"Yeah I know but there's no time for me this way, I can't compromise with fun."

"God you are walking on Vik's footsteps Rachna, beware."

"I have all the time in the world to pursue my dream, what's the hurry?"

She shot up from her bed in a flash. She drank a glass of water. Her sketches that she was making for the Invogue company lay crumpled on the far end of the table.

"God what am I doing?" She shook her head.

She remembered Raghav's last words. "I wish I had started pursuing my dream a day earlier, at least I could have seen how it fared, I guess I was late."

Suddenly she got the answers to all her questions. The confusion and anxiety in her mind vanished. She got up from her bed and looked at the calendar. It had been four weeks since Niel had offered her the proposal.

"Good so I'm still left with two weeks to complete these designs." She uttered. She cursed herself for the last two weeks that she had wasted. Nevertheless, she promised herself she would do her best to complete the designs within the next two weeks. "Raghav was right, life is too short, I can't delay my dream any longer."

She switched off the lights and prepared for sleep. 'So tomorrow I'll resume what I had left two weeks back' she thought.

Five minutes later, the lights of her room were on and she was sitting on the chair.

She was preparing her designs.

⁂

After bidding goodbye to Ruheen and losing a dear friend in Raghav, Purnima had become a bit serious about life. People around her noticed she thought more than she spoke. Even her self - obsessiveness had receded.

"Things don't just happen, you make them happen." Raghav's words had left an indelible mark on her. She had never thought of life, her future, just flew with the wind. But now she wasn't the same. She worked full throttle to live her life as best as possible. Sometime, somewhere she had decided to do something. But the next instant she forgot about it. Now she was sure she would do it - own a beauty parlour within the next year.

≈

THREE MONTHS LATER................

Vik's mother was as always very annoyed with him, but this time for other reasons. Earlier he slept more than ten hours in a day and never worked. And now he had completely transformed. He barely slept for four hours a day and had toiled for the last three months to achieve what he had planned. Midway between those months he had lost hope of achieving the same. 'Three months is too little time for this' he thought.

However it enthused him to work all the more hard.

He did.

He finally managed to achieve what he had planned in his allotted three months.

He ended up writing a book which he called *When life tricked me.*

EPILOGUE

The day had finally come for which I had waited long. It was a day I had dreamt of living through innumerable nights. It was the day of my recognition, something I desired perennially.

Today I was being rewarded. But getting to it had been difficult, considering the laidback attitude that I once had towards life.

I thought about the previous year, how time had helped to evolve me as a person I never thought I would be. It had been a revelation in itself. And then I thought about today. I felt ecstatic. The smile on my face somewhat managed to cloak the pain that I was now used to.

I got up from my bed and slouched on my favourite chair. The memories didn't seem to fade away. *One day I'll do something big to make you guys feel proud of me.*

I looked up to the pictures of my friends on the wall. They were all there- Nirvaan, Ruheen, Purnima, Rachna and of course Raghav - my best friend.

It was to him I owed all my success.

An hour later, I left my house for the evening that awaited me.

I was stupefied when I reached Kamani Auditorium. The honour and appreciation I got for my book was overwhelming. Me, Vikram Oberoi aka Vik had been nominated for the best young author for the year 2012. It had taken me days to digest the fact and likewise for my family and friends.

When I reached there, my friends rushed forward to congratulate me.

"Hey Vik," Nirvaan screamed, "you did it man, we are all proud of you."

"Thanks buddy." I said.

"Vik you are really a man of your words." Purnima said, "You proved you do what you say."

"Thanks again." I said.

"Remember Vik," Rachna added "that day when we were sitting at Cumesum in Nizamuddin, when Nirvaan had just returned from his ship."

I nodded.

"That day," she continued "you told us, one of these days I'll do something to make you guys feel proud of me."

"Yeah," I sighed. "I remember that."

"Well tell you what Vik!" Rachna continued in a tone of appreciation, "You have actually made all of us proud, no one had thought that you would become an author and a successful one at that."

"Thanks, thanks guys." I acknowledged.

Even Ruheen had come all the way from Lucknow to congratulate me. I noticed she had changed. She didn't even look at Nirvaan. He, however endeavoured to strike up a conversation with her. But she turned his requests down. She came towards me and smiled. "Vik you did it, your big thing you always spoke about."

It was overwhelming. I had never felt like that in years. I wish Raghav was here. I wanted to hug him. I missed him. A tear trickled down my eyes and I was breathing heavily.

"Hey Vik." Nirvaan held my hand "What happened, why are you crying?"

"So what else do I do?" I shouted, "You think I would have done all this if it wasn't for Raghav."

They all went quiet. They knew I was right. It was actually to Raghav I owed all my success. I couldn't suppress my tears.

An hour later, it was time for the results. There were four authors in all, nominated for the same title. Vikram Oberoi was one of them.

Do I really deserve this?

Me, out of all the people.

Shocking as it was, I was declared the winner. Me, Vikram Oberoi was the best young author. God, I wished, Raghav was here. I pranced towards the stage. From there I could see the crowd in front of me. They had all put their hands together for me. My mother and sisters were elated to say the least. Surely they had never expected such a thing from a hopeless person as me. But they were clapping and crying. I was gratified.

The trophy was handed over to me and yet again the crowd erupted. My name was announced – Vikram Oberoi - Best young author. It felt like a dream. Oh I really wished Raghav were here.

"Your message for the youth." One of the members of the jury handed over the mike to me.

Me! I am a prick. What message can I give to the youth.

The crowd was waiting. They wanted to hear from me. "For six years I said I'll do something big one day, but it took me just three months to achieve my big thing once I decided it, so guys decide what you want, that's the first step towards the life you have always dreamt of. And decide today, now, because life is short, really short, you have to be on your toes if you want to achieve something in life."

And then tears came rolling down my eyes.